summer love

LARA ALSPAUGH

BLUE WATER BAY
BOOK 1

All rights reserved. No part of this publication may be reproduced, distributed, or transmitted in any form or by any means, including photocopying, recording, or other electronic or mechanical methods, without the prior written permission of the publisher, except in the case of brief quotations embodied in critical reviews and certain other noncommercial uses permitted by copyright law.

This novel is a work of fiction. Names, characters, places, and incidents either are the product of the author's imagination or are used fictitiously.

© 2022 Lara Alspaugh

ISBN: 978-1-7337678-3-5

Book design and editing by Poole Publishing Services LLC

OTHER BOOKS BY LARA ALSPAUGH

Last Turn Home

Love, Red

True North Series:

Where the Beauty Is

Forget Me Not

DEDICATION

Andrea Rowe-Tighe
September 6, 1973 - July 31, 2021

You believed in my strength and courage when I needed you to.

I promise to always dance when I hear Prince. And even when I don't.

Love you always

Lar xoxo

"I wonder what it would be like to live in a world where it was always June." — L.M. Montgomery

Sue,

much love ♡

[signature]
xo

Chapter 1

1988

"It's right there!" He pointed his long, tan arm up toward the black sky.

"Right where?" She laughed.

"The three stars together? In a little line? That's Orion's belt."

"Oh! I see it now! Wait, I think I do?" She laughed again. "I've been staring at the sky so hard, trying to find them, that my eyes are seeing stars where there aren't any and none where there ... are."

He chuckled and squeezed her hand.

"What else can you see?" she asked.

"Umm ... nothing. That's the only one I know! Well that and the big dipper, obviously. But a big ice cream scoop in the sky is not as impressive as a hunter from Greek mythology. So, I only bring out the belt when I'm trying to impress."

Her lips slid up on the left side, giving him a halfway

smile he couldn't resist.

When he stopped walking, she continued, waiting to turn around until their arms were stretched as far as they could be without letting go of each other. He watched her shoulders rise up and slope down as she took a deep breath before she turned again in his direction. She walked slowly toward him, the small distance taking just a moment.

He gathered her up in his arms, pulling her small frame into his taller, stronger one. For a moment he simply rested his chin on the top of her head, tucking her in next to him as tightly as he could. It was she who pulled away, arching her back to lift her face up toward his.

He bent to meet her, their lips whispering against each other at first. A gentle, chaste touch. Someone watching would wonder if it was their first kiss. Her arms reached up around his neck as she stretched to her tiptoes, meeting the second kiss with more desire.

They stayed that way for a while, his hands gliding across her back and hers holding on to his neck. The sun had long set on the day and nearly closed on summer. Time held still beneath the inky black sky, suspended somewhere between now and then.

Walking again, a rogue wave slipped up past the strandline the surf had left on the beach earlier in the day, soaking their bare feet. They let the wave come and go, and another after that. He held on to her hand, she held his back tightly. There wasn't much left to say after the summer they spent together. Especially now that it was over.

"Are you excited to go back to school?" she asked.

"Are you?" he answered.

Her eyes sparkled by the light of the half moon while she shook her head *no*. She was beautiful. Her small stature gave you the feeling she needed protecting, and he supposed there was something to that. But the truth was, she was strong enough on her own. It's one of the things he loved about her.

He wriggled his hand out of hers, catching a sideways glance of dislike. He smirked and slung his arm around her shoulders instead and spun her back down the beach the way they came.

When they got back to their spot, she busied herself by shaking off the sand that had blown up on the beach blanket they'd left out and straightening it again. He stacked the logs he'd brought from his parents' shed into a fire teepee, shoving wrinkled newspaper in the space underneath. The match sizzled as he struck it. They watched together as the small flame slowly, surely, engulfed the paper and then the logs.

"Do you think anybody can see us?" she asked. Her

brows knitted together with a hint of worry.

"Nah. We're far enough back here. Besides, it's Monday night. Nobody will be out and about."

He walked back to his Mustang and returned with his dad's green Coleman cooler and a boombox. "I taped the countdown earlier. Do you want to listen to it?"

She nodded. He pulled the cassette out of his jean jacket pocket—September was in the air—and plopped it into the player. His fingers hit rewind to be sure it started at the beginning, waiting until the backward whirring stopped before he pushed play.

When the music started, he reached behind the boombox into the Coleman and pulled out two wine coolers. "I know the peach is your favorite," he said while he popped the tops off of each bottle, handing her the one that felt the coldest from the ice.

She took a long drink, tipping her head back toward the sky.

"I can't believe summer is over already," she said.

For a moment he thought she might cry. He'd seen her cry twice this summer. Once when her dad moved out, and once when she'd had a fight with her friend Maggie. It wasn't that he wanted to see her upset, but he couldn't help but hope he meant enough to her that she might.

"Oh I forgot something!" she said, jumping up from her spot just as he was sitting down. He watched her run back to his car and pull her backpack out, then carry it to the blanket.

He laughed as soon as he saw the two Hershey's chocolate bars, a small bag of marshmallows, and a box of graham crackers.

"S'mores!" she announced.

They ate marshmallows and drank wine coolers and sang along to their favorite songs, fast-forwarding through the commercials. When they were done eating, they washed their sticky hands off in the cold lake water. The September air blew in with an edge of fall, and the pair cuddled up together as night fell hard.

"Are you cold?" he asked. He could feel her trembling beside him.

"No, I'm not cold," she answered.

He pulled his arms around her tightly, holding her close. "Are you sure?" he asked again. "I think I have another blanket and maybe a sweatshirt in the car."

She shook her head *no* in response. "It's not the cold … I don't want you to leave," she whispered, her voice barely rising above the rumble of the waves on the sand.

"I don't want to leave, either. I'd stay right here forever if we could."

"Why can't we?" she said, knowing the answer.

Summer Love

They hadn't talked about a future, or what would happen when he wasn't in Blue Water Bay anymore. Instead, they had both just *known* September was the end. Theirs was a summer love. Still, he held her tightly, remembering the rise and fall of her chest as she took jagged breaths in and out, trying not to cry.

"Do you promise not to forget me?" she said.

"I could never forget you." His eyes wandered up to the stars, wishing they would have aligned.

Chapter 2

Olivia Pennington looked out her kitchen window at the cerulean-blue water that stretched out into the horizon. Lake Huron was the bluest water north of the Caribbean. It sparkled this morning, the sun glinting off the tip of each wave, mapping a constellation of stars in the water. The second largest great lake, Lake Huron could be temperamental. But this morning there was nothing but sunshine and a sense of easy sailing.

The exact opposite of how Olivia felt.

She walked around her kitchen island, running her hands along the countertop, then tucked a lock of her pixie-cut hair behind her ear. Her computer, which she had relocated from her office in hopes of stirring some sort of writer's block antidote, sat open, a blank page staring back at her. She took a deep breath, and then another, before taking a second lap around the island to avoid sitting down. It was impossible not to hear the leaky faucet, *drip-drip-drip,* or notice the paint peeling around the window sill. Her eyes caught every imperfection. Liv sighed and sat back down on the uncomfortable stool she'd stationed herself at.

"Okay, Liv. Take a deep breath. Just … write." She obediently lifted her hands to her keyboard, poised in QWERTY typing pose—as she'd been taught by Mrs. Nixon in the ninth grade. And … nothing. Quite literally, nothing. Her brain was as empty as the file sitting in front of her. Book One in her highly anticipated happily-ever-after romance series was in trouble.

And so was she.

For most of her life, writing came easily. In fact, it wasn't just easy, it was fun. Characters sprang to life from small nuggets of inspiration she got from people watching and—if she was being honest—eavesdropping on interesting conversations. Life in her imaginary worlds unfolded easily, and her characters gave her the opportunity to see life through a different lens. No day at work could be boring when every day was spent in a different world of her imagination.

But it wasn't like that anymore.

That morning started much like this one. Her coffee was black, as always, and his flavored with a splash of cream. They watched the sunrise, enough time and love between them to sit comfortably in silence. Once the sun had risen and the peaceful mystique of the beginning of the day had faded, they talked about everything and nothing.

Michael had been so excited about their daughter Bella's track meet scheduled for that night. As a junior in high school, she was favored to win regionals and likely the state championship. Liv had listened halfheartedly as he dissected his favored strategy for Bella to win the race. Liv had wanted Bella to do well, of course, but talking about the race made her nervous, so she nodded and listened while she mentally checked off the list of things she was in charge of: clean uniform, cooler packed with water, and Bella's favorite race day snacks. *Check, check, check.*

Michael's voice rose as he anticipated the evening. His excitement was contagious, but Liv was preoccupied. Her thoughts drifted to her newest book—the first in a new series called *Lover's Cove*. It wasn't due until the next spring so she had plenty of time to plan. She twisted the plot around in her mind like a piece of taffy, trying to find the perfect angle. It was the curse of being a writer; her characters were never far from her mind and she easily slipped into other worlds when she should have been paying attention.

They had been together since they were teenagers. For so long they had been Liv and Michael, Michael and Liv, that even now, two years later, the fact that she is just *Liv* didn't seem real. Standing up again, Liv shook her head to dislodge the sadness and picked up her phone. Bella had exams this morning so she shot off a quick text of encouragement to her daughter and then sat back down, returning to her computer.

Liv had not always wanted to be a mother, but Michael had been born to be a father. When the time came, they had compromised on one child. Liv relented because being a parent meant more to Michael than not being a parent meant to Liv. In the end, once Liv held her tiny Bella—born a month early—in her arms, the love she had for her daughter consumed her.

Guilt was a powerful motivator, and from the moment Bella was born Liv had given her best effort to be a good mother. She worked to make up for any lack of desire she once felt toward motherhood with total commitment to her new role. While Michael grew his construction company, Olivia dutifully put her just-budding career on simmer until Bella hit school age.

It was true Michael was the more natural—and nurturing—parent of the two. His instincts for caring for their daughter came easily, while Liv sometimes labored over what to do. When Bella cried, she almost always preferred her daddy. While at first it hurt Liv—wasn't every child supposed to *want* their mother?—

Michael comforted Liv along with Bella. It was *good* for Bella to be close to them both. And she was, just in different ways.

Eventually Liv settled into a comfortable sense of peace that she and Michael made strong co-parents. She excelled at the "motherment" of parenthood—managing Bella's schedule, providing well-rounded learning and development opportunities, running committees and volunteering in class. And Michael kissed boo-boos, talked her through the middle school mean girls, and as she grew, he was her guardian to any and all boys who showed interest. They were a team, and they were happy.

The morning of the track meet Liv finished her coffee first and headed upstairs to dress for her own morning run. She threw on a pair of black leggings, a teal T-shirt, and a white sweatshirt. She tugged on her new black running shoes, kissed Michael goodbye, and headed out the door.

Three miles later, she'd returned with the next scene percolating in her mind as quickly as her morning coffee had brewed. She'd burst in the back door and taken the stairs to their bedroom two by two, pulling her sweatshirt over her head as she moved. Michael used to joke she was an overfull pitcher of water: new ideas, characters, or plot points all sloshing over the edges, soaking everything in its way.

And so she'd been distracted by her imagination. She hadn't noticed Michael's car still in the driveway or that his shoes were still lined up carefully by the back door. Even as she came upon Michael lying on the floor of their master bathroom, sprawled across the cold tile floor, his arms held in awkward angles against his body, she didn't understand that in that moment everything had changed.

Weeks later, the autopsy would reveal that he'd had a widowmaker heart attack. She'd been told, by everyone who knew, that there was nothing she could have done. He was gone in an instant. He hadn't known. He hadn't suffered. Still, she had trouble wrapping her mind—or perhaps her heart—around the simple truth that *she* hadn't just known the second it happened. How could his heart *stop* and hers continue to beat?

She looked out the kitchen windows at the great expanse of blue water, her favorite distraction from her empty page, and watched a freighter pass by. Michael had loved the massive shipping vessels that sailed by their house on their routes. There were so many things that reminded Liv of her husband, it seemed she couldn't turn her head in this old house and not see him. There was nowhere to look to forget that he simply *wasn't* there.

Liv would never put down the subtle weight of Michael's absence. She carried it over her shoulders like a heavy wool coat. It was the least she could do, since she had been the one left living.

That wool coat stayed with her in the winter when the snow fell, and in the fall when the leaves turned brilliant orange and red with rust. It hung on her small frame when the daffodils bloomed and when the warmth of the summer sun melted her hard winter angles like butter. She had grown comfortable under the weight of her sadness. Carrying it felt nearly effortless, and was easier than the thought of setting it down. Setting it down would feel too close to forgetting him, and that she could not do.

Of course it had occurred to her that this, Michael's death, was the reason for her writer's block. In a comical—or perhaps more accurately *ironic*—plot twist, Liv couldn't find the words she needed to move on with *Lover's Cove,* but she began to narrate her life in her mind as if she were a character in the novel.

Liv had been so traumatized by finding her husband dead on the floor that she was unable to go on.

Liv went about her days, running, drinking coffee, simply moving one foot in front of the other without any particular forward motion.

Liv existed in a fog, as thick as pea soup.

Summer Love

It seemed the only words Liv could write were in her head. It wasn't fair that she'd lost the love of her life. Shouldn't she be able to keep her work? Work was supposed to be where she escaped. Work was supposed to be where she forgot the fact that her husband, her very best friend, the love of her life was gone. Instead, work was where she became the biggest failure of all.

For the first six months after Michael died, she'd simply put one foot in front of the other. She didn't write. She didn't answer emails or do book events. She didn't do writing retreats or author panels or interviews. She paid the bills with money from savings, Michael's life insurance (which hadn't been much), and the advance she'd received for her upcoming series. She wrote thank you notes for the casseroles people left on her doorstep. She showered and dressed (almost) every day. And she even had lunch with her best friends Frannie, Maggie, and Lucy once a week ("Whether you feel like it or not," Lucy would say—which was good because Liv never, ever felt like it).

Isla, her agent, had gone to bat for her, putting up her own word for collateral with her publisher and brokered a generous contract extension—a grace period of an extra year to deliver her next book.

Two years should have been plenty of time to pick up where she'd left off the morning Michael died. But somewhere underneath the heavy wool coat, the tiny sprite of a woman who had been a force of action and decision had changed. So she did what she could and she spent her days managing the taxing and complicated work of living. And she didn't write a word.

After the first six months passed, Liv still wasn't interested in writing. Her focus was sketchy at best, and there were no plot lines that could catch her attention enough for her to stay committed for more than a few thousand words before she trashed them. Instead, she traded her writing for a different singular focus—to help Bella win the state championship Michael had been so excited about before he died. She hadn't run that race, but she had one more chance at the end of her senior year.

Later that spring, a year after Michael died, she did it. Bella won.

They had done it—watching her girl reach the finish line *first* was everything she had focused on. It was everything Liv had counted on to bring her back to life. Liv had been desperate to feel joy for the first time since Michael had stopped breathing. Liv had hoped to *feel* Michael there with them, in truth she had *expected* it.

But it hadn't happened.

As Olivia stood in the pouring rain that had complicated the race and watched the gold medal hung around her daughter's neck, she'd felt … nothing. Nothing from Michael. Even her pride in Bella—which academically she knew was enormous—felt soft around the edges. She'd been hoping for a bright firework of emotion, a spark to warm her enough to finally shrug off the wool coat. But it hadn't happened. That was when she realized she would never be the same. That nothing would ever be *normal*, and her wool coat… well, it was there to stay.

Having counted so completely on the race bringing her back to life, Liv wasn't sure what to do when it was over. So, she did the only thing she knew how. She put one foot in front of the other, and focused solely on Bella.

Liv planned graduation activities, shopped for prom dresses, and helped Bella sort through college applications—and scholarship offers. Of which there were many, including one to Michael's alma mater, the University of Michigan. Liv was proud—and insistent—that Bella carry on Michael's legacy.

In just a few days, in time for Memorial Day Weekend and Blue Water Bay's Kickoff to Summer Festival, Bella would return home for the summer after her freshman year at U of M. Liv was both excited and nervous to have Bella home. She knew how much changed in a year—especially your first year away from home. Even so, it would be nice to have another heartbeat in the house, and the Kickoff to Summer Festival was one of Liv's favorite events of the year. In the late months of winter and grueling start of spring, it gave her something to look forward to.

Now, the grandfather clock in the front hallway chimed 10:30 am—a delicate, brassy sound that was as much a part of their home as the matchstick ceiling on the three seasons porch. Liv sighed as she looked back at the computer. She had made no headway. No words. No word count. No progress to report. Which, while obviously a problem, was an even bigger problem as she realized there were now three unread messages from Isla in her inbox. Five in twenty-four hours, seeing that she'd deleted two from yesterday. She hovered her cursor over the unread messages in turn. One sent at 2:23 yesterday afternoon, one sent at 8:46 last night, and one at 10:07 this morning. Liv closed her email without reading any of them and returned to the blank, open document that *was* Book One and felt sick.

That feeling only got stronger when she checked her phone and realized there were two texts from Isla as well.

Isla: Liv! Excited to hear how Book One is coming.

Isla: Call me, please. We need to work on the timeline

for production and I had a spectacular idea for the next series!

Isla wasn't just her editor. She was her friend. And her friend had gone out of her way to protect her after Michael's death. Liv had never, ever missed a deadline. Not in the fifteen years they'd worked together. In fact, she'd almost always come in early. She'd had no reason to believe this writer's block would last so long, so she hadn't told Isla she was struggling. The truth was she was embarrassed she'd had such a generous period of time to write and she didn't have anything to offer. Liv glanced at her phone again, her stomach turning over on itself. How was she supposed to tell Isla there was no need for a production timeline because there was no book?

Without another thought, Liv deleted both texts and went to her bedroom to change her clothes. Writer's block wasn't incurable. She knew how to write, and it was still inside her, she knew it. There had to be an answer. The fact was, she was becoming increasingly sure that she knew what the answer was. She just didn't like it.

Pulling on a white maxi dress printed with small daisies and a slim-cut jean jacket, she ran her fingers through her short, blonde hair, took a quick moment to add mascara and a swipe of blush to her cheeks, and grabbed her cellphone off the bathroom counter. Scanning the contacts until she found who she was looking for, she pushed send before she could change her mind.

"Hello?" The thick southern drawl came through loud and clear, even over the crackle of her sketchy Blue Water Bay cell phone service.

"Hey. It's Liv. I need your help."

Chapter 3

Bella pulled her car over into a parallel parking spot in front of Beyond Blooms. She tipped her head back on the headrest while she closed her eyes and covered her face with her hands. She was exhausted. The past month in Ann Arbor had been excruciating. College had proven to be more difficult than she anticipated. Actually, that is making the assumption she had thought about what college would be like. She hadn't thought past getting out of town.

Taking a deep breath, she pulled her tired body out of her Jeep Cherokee—a gift from her parents for her sixteenth birthday. Bella shook her head to dislodge the thought of her father, the day he gave her the keys. *Funny how people do that*, she thought. As if shaking her head could stop the sadness from coming. It always came. No matter what she did—or didn't do.

Walking to the front door, Bella noticed a blue, rusty Chevy parked in the employee parking lot to the side of The Local Cup. *Hannah.* Bella's stomach turned over at the thought of her former best friend.

When Bella arrived on campus last August, everything was new and exciting. Her new home had begun to feel like the answer to all of her problems. She could start over, taking just the pieces with her she wanted to keep. She could be Fun Bella. Happy Bella. Not … Sad Bella. She didn't have to tell anyone about her dad, so she didn't have to see the flash of pity in their eyes before they forgot about it and moved on. But leaving the old Bella behind meant she had to cut ties with anyone close to the real Bella … like Hannah.

It didn't take long for her to realize that it didn't matter where she lived or how she started over, she had brought Sad Bella with her. She had wanted to talk to Hannah, her oldest and dearest friend. The one who knew her the best—the one who *knew* Sad Bella. But Bella was embarrassed by how she'd treated Hannah, and she was afraid Hannah would never forgive her for blowing her off. So, she didn't reach out and lived with not knowing instead of the certainty of being turned away. Seeing Hannah's car gave Bella an ache deep in her heart, and suddenly she wasn't sure coming home was the right answer.

The problem was, it was her only option.

"Hey, Maggie! Hi, Kevin!"

"Well hello there, Bella! Nice to see you back."

Summer Love

Maggie's right-hand man smiled at Bella.

"Bella! What a surprise, my favorite college co-ed! How are you, kiddo?" Maggie walked out from behind the counter and hugged her best friend's daughter. Immediately Bella felt comforted by Maggie's generous arms around her and sunk into the warmth, her exhaustion taking over.

"I'm good. Tired. How are things here at the shop? How are the boys?" Bella rested her head on Maggie's shoulder for a minute before straightening up and taking a walk about the store. Maggie had a knack; she was the Joanna Gaines of Blue Water Bay, and Bella loved the creativity and small-town feel of the store. It felt like home as much as anywhere, and that helped Bella relax.

Beyond Blooms wasn't just filled with flowers, it was full of sweet-smelling candles, local artists' paintings and photographs on the walls, a collection of gifts, and even a new line of bakeware in the corner. Bella loved everything about Beyond Blooms, but especially Maggie. She was softer somehow than her own mom—and not quasi-famous either. Even now, as Maggie stood sifting through receipts at the front counter, she had a splash of coffee down her front and a pen stuck haphazardly in her blonde curls, which were piled high on top of her head. She *looked* like a mom. She *felt* like a mom. Bella wasn't sure why that was important to her, but it was.

"The shop is good! I have a wedding this weekend—total bridezilla. But, I am working on all of her changes and I think I can make it all work and get it delivered before the Summer Kickoff Party this weekend! The boys are crazy. Crazy good. Crazy loud. Crazy fun. Crazy naughty. All of the above!" Maggie laughed and put her hands on her hips. "I bet your mom was so happy to see you!"

"I haven't gone home yet," Bella answered without meeting Maggie's eyes. Instead, she continued to tour the displays, picking up candles and smelling them, inspecting a potted succulent and trying on a bracelet made from sea glass found on the beach.

"Hmm … you didn't? Well, I'm honored to be your first stop, but your mom has been dying for you to get home for weeks." Maggie let her words drift into quiet. They weren't judgmental, just questioning.

"I just wanted to stop by and see you and the shop. I thought maybe the boys would be here. I can't wait to see them. I bet they have grown so much. I haven't seen them since their spring break when you brought them to my meet." Bella walked toward the flower cooler room and opened the door to take a deep pull in of the gently rose-and tulip-scented air. She stayed there for a moment, her head ducked into the chilled space, pulling herself together before turning around and walking back to the counter.

"They are still at school," Maggie answered while checking her watch, her brow stitched together, squinting to see the time. "So, speaking of school, how was it? Did you have fun? I know the season was great—your mom kept us all up to date. The boys and I had a lot of fun watching you run, they are already talking about next year!"

Bella's heart fluttered, and her hands got sweaty. She paused and then answered, "It was fun. It was hard. But, I can't wait to come back to work. I can start this weekend if you want?"

"Your mom would be pretty upset with me if I asked you to work this weekend. It's the Kickoff to Summer Festival, remember? She's super excited to have you home for it. You know she loves it."

"Yeah, I guess it slipped my mind." Bella's voice was quiet.

"Bella. What's up?"

Bella hesitated, looking around the shop to be sure there were no customers close by and Kevin was out of earshot. Without warning, her eyes filled with tears, and she blurted out, "I dropped out of school."

"What do you mean, you dropped out of school?

You just got home from school." Maggie's eyes grew as big as saucers.

"I finished this semester. But I decided I'm not going back."

"Honey. Honey, honey, honey, what about track? What about your scholarship? What about … school?"

"I told the coach I quit. I can't do it. It's too hard and I don't like it and I just can't …" Bella started to cry in earnest.

"Oh hey, hold on, kiddo." Maggie once again put her arms around Bella and pulled her close. "It's okay. You are okay. I'm sure you and your mom will figure everything out. I'm surprised she hasn't told me yet. Let's go back to my office, okay?"

Bella nodded and wiped her tears away from her cheeks, although more were falling.

"Kevin? Can you hold down the floor for a few minutes?"

"You bet, boss," he answered.

Maggie walked Bella through the store and into her small, cubbyhole of an office. Papers were piled high on the desk, and she had samples of ribbon, tule, and gems sitting on the side counter. Bella picked up a slip of ribbon left over from a bouquet and ran it through her fingers. It felt good to have something to do with her hands.

"You can sit in that chair right there, Bella. Just put those catalogs on the floor," Maggie said as she pulled her chair out from behind her desk to sit next to Bella.

When they both were settled and Bella had dried her tears with some Kleenex Maggie had handed her, Bella began to talk.

"My mom doesn't know. And you can't tell her, Maggie. You can't." Bella's tears threatened to return.

Maggie rubbed Bella's back and waited before answering.

"Bella, that's hardly something you can keep from your mom. Don't you think she'll notice when you are still here in August?" Maggie's lips turned down on the corners in sympathy.

"I'm going to tell her. I will. I just need some time. I need to wait for the right time. I don't want to ruin my first weekend home and the festival. Can you just give me a few weeks? I promise I will tell her. As soon as I figure out what I'm going to do next. I want to come to her with a plan—you know how my mom loves a plan! I will tell her as soon as I figure out a plan." Bella nodded her head in certainty, hoping it bought her Maggie's silence.

Maggie leaned back and looked at Bella. "Okay, kiddo. I won't tell your mom. Yet."

Bella nodded and let out the breath she was holding.

Being on borrowed time was better than no time. She felt bad for a moment for asking Maggie to keep a secret from her mom. They were best friends, after all.

"But you need to tell her soon. Your mom has known me most of my life. She knows I'm no good at lying."

Bella smiled and nodded again. Good thing she was.

Chapter 4

Liv pulled the door open to her favorite cafe—The Local Cup—and listened to the gentle tinkle of the bell as she walked in. The tables were full this morning. There were a few customers she knew, like Duncan Waldron, the president of the Blue Water Bay Bank, and Sally Hollingsworth, the owner of the jewelry store down the street. Both smiled and waved. They had known Liv since she was a girl. Duncan had been friends with her father, and Michael had bought her wedding ring from the Hollingsworth Jewelry Store. Just as Liv turned to find a table, she noticed Angela Murphy in the corner booth with her computer, presumably working. Liv averted her eyes as quickly as she could. The very last thing she needed this morning was to catch that woman's attention. Angela was the middle-aged version of a middle school mean girl. Her long, blonde hair, longer lean legs, and picture-perfect style gave her a social credit Liv never thought she deserved. Lucy, one of Liv's best friends, and Angela went head-to-head for all of the real estate deals in town. It was well known that Lucy was ethical and hardworking. And Angela was sneaky, willing to tip-toe down a line of moral compromise to seal the deal. On top of that, the woman had a nose for gossip, and she'd like nothing more than to know Liv's secrets.

Liv smiled in the direction of a table of women whom she didn't know, but they smiled at her as if they did. The back of her head burned as their eyes followed her across the room, wondering if she was who they thought she was. After all, Liv was a *New York Times* Best Seller. Just a few months before Michael died, she'd been a guest on *Ellen*, *Good Morning America*, and—her favorite—*Hoda & Jenna*, promoting her last series, *Peace River*. Isla had been a genius at marketing her to mainstream media, and for being a romance author, Liv was something of a big deal.

Being recognized had been a fun afterthought of her choice in career—not something she had expected or had wanted, but a perk nonetheless. Michael had found it thrilling—he was very proud of his wife. Bella, on the other hand, actively disliked when readers approached her mother in public. *No need to worry about that now, Bella! I'm not writing, and no one is reading,* she thought.

The inside of The Local Cup was painted a pale yellow with pops of teal and peacock blue, and was as comfortable and inviting as your grandma's kitchen.

"Hi there, Mrs. Pennington!"

"Well, hello there, Hannah." Liv smiled and opened her arms to give the young woman a hug. "How are you?"

Bella and Hannah had been best friends since middle school—in fact, until Bella went to college, Hannah had been a fixture at the Pennington house. It had been ages since Liv had seen her.

"Is Misty in today?" Misty, the owner of The Local Cup, was responsible for the woodsy, minty-tea smell that mingled with roasted coffee beans and the heavenly scent of an entire cabinet of baked goods. Liv took a deep breath.

"I'm good! No, Misty is out right now. She should be back later. We do have her 'famous' raspberry rolls on special today—I am just getting ready to pull the last pan out of the oven." Hannah smiled as she made air quotes around the word *famous*. With her teal Local Cup baseball hat tucked down over her brown eyes, small wisps of her long brown hair gently framing her face, the familiarity of Bella's best friend made Liv even more excited for Bella's return.

"Well, that sounds delicious. I'll take it. And a coffee too, please? Skim and sugar-free vanilla. Tell Misty I said hello?"

"Of course! How's Bella doing? How was her track season?" Hannah asked as she filled Liv's coffee cup.

"She had a good season, for a freshman in particular. Actually, she will be home this Thursday! Just in time for the Summer Kickoff."

"Oh my gosh, really? That's great! Maybe we'll run into each other this summer." Hannah's voice was sincere.

"Well of course you will see each other! I expect you to be over as soon as she gets home!" Liv smiled.

Hannah hesitated before turning toward the kitchen and answering, "I can bring your order out as soon as it's ready, Mrs. Pennington. Your table is free." She smiled and nodded her head in the direction of the corner before walking away.

It occurred to Liv suddenly that she hadn't heard Bella talk much about Hannah lately. Maybe the girls had a spat, or maybe it was teenagers just not communicating well. Liv couldn't imagine the two—who had always been thick as thieves—drifting too far apart. She made a mental note to check in with Bella about Hannah when she returned home.

Just as Liv sat in the round corner booth—the one

she, Frannie, Maggie and Lucy sat at when they met for their Ladies of the Round Table lunches once a week—she heard the heralding of the tinkle bells and turned to see Frannie.

"Hey, Liv! How ya doin'?"

Liv smiled at Frannie's southern drawl. Frannie, her thick auburn hair pulled back in a low ponytail, was dressed in overall bibs splashed with paint. Her hands, also coated in paint with nails trimmed short, pulled at her ponytail, tugging it tighter. One would think she'd be anything but feminine—since she was in fact the best handy-woman in town—but they would be wrong. Liv smiled as she could smell her friend approach—sweet, fresh-cut pine with a tinge of rusty metal—and, surprisingly, vanilla. Somehow, it worked on her.

Frannie was a knockout. A true natural beauty with piercing green eyes, a bridge of freckles over her nose, and creamy white skin. Liv had tried to capture Frannie's unique spirit a few times over the years in different characters. Somehow, it never turned out in words as well as Frannie pulled it off in real life.

"I am good. I just ordered. Go ahead and put in an order on my tab. I'll wait. The raspberry rolls are on special."

"Sounds delish!" Frannie answered.

Within a few minutes, Frannie returned with a blueberry scone and a large sweet tea chocked full with four lemon wedges.

"Hannah will bring out your roll in a minute. I can never turn down Misty's scones. So, what do you need my help with?" Frannie asked, her dimples deep and inviting. She took a bite of her blueberry scone first, adding, "I think Misty uses lemon as the secret ingredient. Don't you?"

"I do," Liv answered. "I do think maybe it's lemon and I also do … need your help."

"Well, you know I've been dying to get my hands on that house of yours. I'm assuming you need some repairs or reno work done?" Frannie was cautious with her eyes. Obviously her friends had noticed she'd let some things slide since Michael died.

"Yes, I do. I … well, before I say a word, I need you to keep this private. Between you and me."

"Okay. Not even Lucy and Maggie?" she asked.

"No, not even them. No. One." Liv lowered her eyes to meet Frannie's gaze.

"All right, y'all know a proper southern belle never kisses and tells," Frannie laughed, her full, deep voice settling between the two friends.

"I think I am going to sell the house—"

"*What?*" Frannie nearly yelled. She quickly covered

her mouth with her free hand as Angela turned from her computer and looked in the direction of the two friends. Liv didn't bother to wave, but Frannie did. "You? You are going to sell the house?" she whispered back, leaning deeply toward Liv.

"I'm *thinking* about it, yes. But I have a lot of small projects that need to get done—either way. The house needs painting, and the faucet is leaking in the kitchen. The pantry doorknob fell off about six months ago, and there is a very strange squeak coming from the third stair on the way to my office."

Liv shouldn't have been surprised by Frannie's reaction. Everyone knew she loved her home. She loved the wide plank floors and the old windows that looked out over the bluff from the porch. She loved the fireplace—original to the 1928 house—and loved to imagine all the fires that had taken place before hers, as well as remember the fires she'd spent snuggled with Michael and Bella. And Liv *did* love her house. Liv selling the house doesn't make much sense—unless you are Liv.

Because Liv had tried everything under the sun to cure herself of her writer's block and nothing has worked. The only thing she hadn't tried—the only thing left—was moving away from the house she lived in with Michael. The house where Michael died.

"Okay, I can handle all of those things." Frannie,

not typically at a loss for words, looked directly at Liv and squeezed her eyebrows together. "Why is this a secret?"

Frannie and Liv looked up as Hannah approached the table. "Sorry, it took me an extra minute, the counter got really busy! Here you go." Hannah placed a warm raspberry roll in front of Liv.

"I'm sure it will be worth the wait." She smiled and watched Hannah walk away before turning back to Frannie. "For one, I'm not one-hundred-percent sure I *will* sell." Liv twisted her fingers around each other, working through her nervous energy. She was hoping—*praying*—she wouldn't need to sell. But time was running thin, and she didn't know what else to do.

"Well, then don't. If you don't want to sell, don't. I've worked with plenty of homeowners who paid me to fix up their homes to sell—who almost immediately had seller's remorse once they did. Don't do it." Frannie's emerald-green eyes shone with conviction.

"I don't *want* to sell. I think I *need* to sell," Liv answered, her eyes cast upward.

"Oh … oh … wait a minute. What is this really—"

Liv interrupted her friend, "Frannie. Listen. It's … it's my work." Liv's eyes looked down in her lap before skittering back up to meet Frannie's gaze. Under the table she crossed her fingers together like a schoolgirl did when she was about to lie. She couldn't tell Frannie money was *also* a motive. Michael would be mortified from the grave. He'd worked so hard to give them a comfortable life. And he had. A good life. The best life. Before Michael died, Liv would have never imagined she would be in financial trouble. And she wasn't ... yet. But she would be if she couldn't get this writer's block under control, deliver her manuscript, and get to writing the next book in *Lover's Cove.* She prayed she still had time to save everything she and Michael had created—but if she didn't, she needed to find a solution quickly and quietly.

"Wait ... your work? What does your work have to do with your house?"

"You know, ever since Michael died, I just can't seem to write there. I have writer's block and I really am struggling with it. I was thinking about a new environment ... Maybe a condo would be easier? Maybe that would help? Somewhere with fewer memories, fewer reminders ..." Liv worked to keep her voice light. She had yet to admit to a single person she had writer's block. Telling Frannie the truth felt oddly satisfying.

"You in a condo? Seriously? Darlin', you love that house. It suits you. The history suits you. Are you sure there isn't another answer to this writer's block problem? Come down here and write! Go to the library! You don't *have* to write at home! You can write anywhere."

"Good afternoon, ladies!" Maggie set down her coffee and pumpkin macadamia chocolate chip cookie, then scooted her bottom around the circle booth toward Liv. Her dimples, killer smile, and blonde curls piled on top of her head immediately soothed Liv. Maggie was to Liv as Hannah was to Bella. Besties for life.

"Hi, Maggie." Liv smiled, hoping her friend didn't overhear her conversation. She hadn't seen her coming.

"Hi, Maggie!" Frannie added, her voice louder than needed.

"What are you two up to? I didn't know there was a meeting of the Round Table Ladies." Maggie smiled hesitantly. "Is Lucy here, too?"

"Of course not! We can't have a Ladies of the Round Table Meeting without you and Lucy." Liv smiled and quickly squeezed her friend's hand. "I think Lucy had a showing this afternoon in Franklin? Frannie and I were just talking—I am researching a new character for my book, and Frannie is helping me out."

Frannie took a long pull of her coffee. She winced as she burned her throat by drinking too quickly. Lying to their best friend—or covering up the exact truth, as Liv was looking at it—was not inherently easy or comfortable for either of them, but for Frannie it was downright painful. Putting her friend out of her misery, Liv added, "And she's going to do a couple odds and ends at the house for me. So, we were just getting that squared away."

"What are you out doing, darlin'?" Frannie asked. Maggie owned Beyond Blooms, the only floral shop in town, which happened to be connected to the old building that housed The Local Cup.

"I just needed a quick pick-me-up—I have that huge wedding this coming weekend, remember? Working with Bridezilla and Bridezilla's Mother was bad enough, now Bridezilla's Mother-In-Law-To-Be has decided to throw her weight around. In fact, I have to run—they made a few pretty big changes and I've got to check with a few vendors and see if I can make it all happen."

"Have a floral shop, they said. It will be fun, they said." Liv laughed at Maggie.

Handing out air kisses on each cheek, Maggie quickly picked up her coffee and cookie, waved good-bye to Hannah, and headed back toward Beyond Blooms.

Frannie sat quietly in the corner of the Round Table booth. Her coffee was long gone, and her hands clasped together in prayer as her elbows rested on the table. "So, you don't want me to tell anyone you are selling the house?"

"*Thinking* of selling the house."

"Okay, you don't want me to tell anybody you are *thinking* of selling the house?"

"No. I don't. I cannot let Bella know before I've made a final decision. And Maggie—she works with Bella nearly every day. She might slip."

"What about Lucy? Why can't we tell Lucy?" Frannie was really not liking Liv's secrets.

"I will tell Lucy. Of course, I will tell Lucy. When I'm ready. She'll be the one to list and sell the house. I just … I just need time to get the house ready and wrap my mind around it all and make a final decision. That's it. I don't want to go telling people I am selling and then … change my mind. Can you give me a few weeks of secrecy?" Liv quickly slid her eyes toward Angela.

"I don't like it. But I will," Frannie finally answered. Liv reached over and squeezed her friend's paint-stained hands.

"Thank you. I know it may seem silly. But this writer's block … it's … it's not going away. Frannie, I haven't been able to write at all. Not one word."

"You will figure it out." Frannie smiled and slung her arm around Liv's slight shoulders.

Liv forced a smile and took a bite of her roll as she hid another secret from Frannie.

The big secret.

Her extended—and final—deadline to finish book one in *Lover's Cove* was approaching. And if she didn't make it—she'd have to return the advance she'd been given for this book. The problem was, she didn't *have* the money to return.

Chapter 5

Bella listened to the familiar sound of gravel crunching under her tires as she pulled into her driveway. She was home for the first time in months, and it felt instantly both lonely and comforting. It's hard to be homesick, harder to be homesick when nowhere feels like home. Taking a deep breath, she opened her car door, the breeze was warm with just a hint of early summer chill off the big lake. Her dad used to call Lake Huron "the big icebox" in the dead of winter. It always took a while to warm up, and while it did, their days were cooler here on the water.

She walked toward the house, taking note of the big oak that shaded both the driveway and the south side porch. Her dad had taken her picture next to the tree every first day of school from kindergarten until … well until he wasn't there to take another picture. Bella squeezed her eyes tight. Damnit. Sad Bella was all she knew how to be anymore.

Three freighters were stationed out in the distance.

She loved to see the big ships on the horizon. Somehow, the industrial monstrosities felt romantic in a weird way. Bella and Hannah used to ride jet skis out to jump the freighter waves. Something her dad thought was awesome and her mom hated. Riding along the huge waves so close to the ships made Bella feel small, but in a good way. A way that reminded her of who she was and where she was from. It reminded her how big the world was. Back then it felt exciting. It felt like anything was possible.

She sighed, wishing life was that simple again. Now, nothing felt exciting, and things felt more *impossible* instead of possible. Missing her dad was like a spilled glass of water—it seeped into everything.

"It's now or never," she whispered to herself. Her body felt achy, tired. During the past few months at school, trying to keep up with classes and practices was hard. She couldn't wait to climb upstairs, crawl into her own familiar bed, and sleep. Maybe she'd stay there for a week. Then she remembered her back seat. She'd thrown everything from her dorm room in at once. No packing, no organizing. It would take her hours of work to unpack and organize the mess she'd made.

"Hey, Mom. You home?" she asked as she walked through the side door. It was a redundant question. She had seen her mom's car in the driveway, and it was way too late in the afternoon for her to be on a run. If Bella knew her mom at all, she was up in her office writing. Her mom was a lot of things, predictable being at the top of the list.

"Bella? Bella, is that you?" her mom called from somewhere upstairs.

Bella shook her head. Bingo. She was in her office. "Yep, I'm home." Bella tried to echo the joyful sentiment she knew her mom wanted to hear.

"You're early!" Liv practically yelled as her footsteps tic-tacked down the stairs. "Let me see you, sweet pea." Liv wrapped Bella up in a hug, her small arms reaching clear around her daughter's neck. The pair stood quietly for a moment, Liv kissing Bella on the forehead.

Bella was the one to pull away. She was a practical kid, more like her mom than she wanted to admit. Lavish displays of emotion, particularly from Liv, were uncomfortable.

"You look so thin, Bella. Are you hungry? Do you want to eat? Do you need help carrying your stuff in? I said I would come help you on Thursday; why didn't you wait—"

"Mom. Mom. Mom. Take a breath. For goodness' sake. Can we take it one question at a time, please?" Although she tried to keep it calm—she *really* didn't want to fight with her mom in the first five minutes—

Bella's voice came out with an edge.

Liv reached up and tucked her hair behind her ears. "Yep. Yep we can. I'm sorry. I'm just so happy to have you here." Liv stepped away and walked toward the fridge. "How about we start with some lunch? I was just getting ready to eat myself."

"I'm not super hungry, but I guess I can eat a little."

Liv pulled out four hard-boiled eggs, avocado, mayo, and a loaf of rye bread. "I can make egg salad sandwiches and I have a quart of early strawberries, too. From Holly's Strawberry Farm. Sound good?"

"Sure, I guess. I'm not super hungry, like I said." Actually, it sounded heavenly. Dorm food was atrocious, and she had never been a kid who liked fast food. A simple, basic home-prepared meal would be wonderful. She wasn't sure why she couldn't gift her mom with the kindness of happily accepting the meal—she just couldn't.

"I had your carpets cleaned and I washed all your linens on your bed—your room is all ready for you for the summer. When do you go back again? The third week in August?"

Bella took a long swig of the lemonade Liv had poured her—feigning thirst—as she prepared herself to answer. "I don't know, Mom. I just got done. Can I please have an hour at home before you prepare to ship me off again?" Setting the glass down harder than needed, Bella walked into the other room, seemingly to use the bathroom. Although once she rounded the corner and shut the door behind her, Bella took a deep breath and looked at herself in the mirror. She knew she should tell her mom the truth. She even knew she would feel better if she did. But somehow, Bella couldn't find the words. The truth is hard, and lying... well, lying is so much easier.

Bella's stomach clenched again, feeling tight and twisted. Rejoining her mom at the table, she pasted a smile on her face and sat down to eat her lunch so she could take a nap. Surely if she complied for a little while, her mom would leave her be.

"So, how's the book coming? Isn't your deadline like September or something?"

Liv put her hands to her mouth as she slowly chewed. "Yep, it's due first of September. It's going well ... trying to round out some plot points before I send it to a few beta readers. That will probably be next week. So it will be out of my hair for a little bit—which is good because I planned a few day trips for us to—"

"Mom, I have to work. Did you forget?" Why did everything Bella say come out with razor-sharp teeth?

"No, no I didn't forget. In fact, when I saw Maggie earlier today we talked about it. I know you are excited, but you won't work every day all summer. Beyond Blooms isn't even open on Sundays! So I figured we could go then."

"I do have a life, you know. I have friends and things I want to do—on my own. And you'll have your book to work on, so I didn't really plan on a lot of day trips. Plus, I just got home. I want to be home for a while." Why in the world was Bella being so mean? If she was honest, she would have said some day trips sounded fun—maybe Mackinac Island or Cedar Point, or both. But no matter what her heart felt, her mouth filtered it through a sieve of negativity.

"Oh, okay. Well, I didn't write anything in ink. So, if you are free, just let me know and we can do something fun. Doesn't have to be big. Maybe just a trip to the beach for the afternoon?" Liv's enthusiasm was gone.

"I just really need to sleep, Mom," Bella answered.

"I get it. Why don't you go get a nap and I will clean this up. I can help you unpack and bring everything in when you wake up."

Bella thought of the haphazard mess in her car, the unwashed clothes and dirty dishes mixed in with copies of failing term papers. "No, no I can do it. It's fine. I just need a nap first." The last thing she needed was her mom's help. It would only lead to Liv asking questions, and that was the last thing Bella wanted.

Chapter 6

The townspeople of Blue Water Bay were sprawled out on the lawn of the yacht club and marina. They spilled over into the streets that were blocked off and down the docks toward the slips filled with boats. Dressed in red, white, and blue, and sporting stars and stripes, people waved and smiled, shared hugs and handshakes. The Kickoff to Summer Festival was off to a rousing start.

Michigan winters were a strange duality—long, gray, wet, snowy, and cold but also breathtakingly beautiful, eerie and insular in what could be a healing and restful way. No matter how you saw winter, summer was the sweet spot. The time of year when the lakes and rivers and beaches of the mitten state were put to good use, and people came out from behind their coats, gloves, and doors to enjoy each other's company. And Blue Water Bay was no exception. Liv always laughed that Michigan would be California if the weather were good—the landscape was gorgeous, the water salt-free, and the summers were treasured.

"Cash. Carson. Do not let me tell you again. Sparklers are *not* to be used as weapons. I will throw the rest of them in the lake if you can't stop." Maggie used her best *I'm serious* tone of voice while her twins proceeded to snicker and hold their very lit sparklers behind their backs. "I'm not taking you to the hospital if you poke each other's eyes out. I'm not. You'll just have to get yourselves some eye patches and change your names to Hook."

"They really are heathens, aren't they?" Lucy asked, a smirk pinching the sides of her cheeks. After all, she'd been the one to bring the little heathens the sparklers to begin with. Lucy was childless and single by choice, enjoying a free-traveling, free-flinging existence that included spoiling her best friends' twins within an inch of decency. Bella, too.

"They will both be taller than me. Their fluffy momma doesn't wield a very big stick. I don't know what I will do in a few years. They really need their dad to step up. Then again, my life is much easier not dealing with Bruce and Cali," Maggie whispered, turning her voice away from her sons as she poured herself a glass of Liv's spiked lemonade.

"If I have told you once, I have told you a hundred times, do not use the word 'fluffy' to describe my best friend. Full-figured. Curvy. Curvaceous! Any of the above. Just not fluffy. You are not fluffy. Also, is he still being a pain?" Lucy asked.

"My lawyer has me keeping detailed records of missed visitations. He's hoping he can get me a pinch more in child support. Bruce has missed the last three Tuesdays and the weekend in-between. As of today, he hasn't seen the boys in three weeks."

"What a jerk," Bella answered.

"Bella, careful." Liv slid her eyes toward the boys, holding her finger to her lips as she spoke in her daughter's direction.

Bella rolled her eyes at her mom. Liv understood the message; the boys were the ones being ditched and Bella wasn't wrong. Still, Liv didn't want Bella's comment to hurt the boys. Bruce was still their dad. Jerk or not. She smiled back at her daughter, but Bella just turned away.

"There are cheese and crackers, some summer sausage and grapes in the picnic basket as well if anybody would like. I also snuck a few pumpkin white chocolate macadamia nut cookies in there from The Local Cup." Liv picked up the thermos of lemonade she'd packed. "Lucy, do you want another lemonade?"

"I'll take some lemonade, Mom," Bella said.

"Ha ha funny," Liv answered. "You're not legal yet,

missy."

Bella rolled her eyes again at Liv following the rules and picked up her phone, diving straight back into social media. Something was going on with her, Liv just wasn't sure what it was. She'd tried to get her daughter to open up, asking Bella a few vague questions—which were mostly answered by single-word answers or no answer at all. She supposed she should give her more space. Bella had spent the last nine months on her own. She tried to remember how hard it was to go home once she'd left—but that was different. Liv and her mother *never* saw eye-to-eye. In fact, Liv's mom had lived to tell Liv what to do and how to do it. Liv had made great efforts to not repeat that mistake with her daughter. But now she wasn't sure she had done enough.

Liv looked around at her small circle of friends. Since Michael died, she sometimes felt unlucky, even when she knew she was luckier than most in the friendship department. Maggie, Lucy, and Liv had gone to school together since the fifth grade—Maggie was a Blue Water Bay Lifer while Liv and Lucy both moved to the small town the summer they turned ten. Frannie, five years younger, had moved north with her now ex-husband Hank. Lucy had hired Frannie to do some repairs at a rental she managed. With her southern drawl and easy smile she'd fit like the last piece of their puzzle. Now the women prided themselves on the fact that their friendship had weathered the heady stuff life stacks upon you—like divorce, infidelity, death. Rambunctious sons and teenage daughters. They had been through it all together.

"Is Frannie coming?" Bella asked, looking up from her phone for a second. "I haven't seen her yet."

"She's on her way." Lucy lifted her phone up as she spoke, indicating she'd just heard from her.

With just a dusting of sunlight left before the day drew to a close, Liv closed her eyes and let the warm breeze comfort her. It was good to be outside. It was nights like these Liv could feel nearly normal, for a few moments at least. As if the past two years of her life hadn't happened and perhaps Michael was just away on business, or fishing with his father. Liv realized how ridiculous it sounded—her husband had been gone for 774 days, and her father-in-law died before Bella was born. Still, it was comforting to sit inside her imagination and pretend.

The parade was magnificent, as small-town parades go. It had kicked off with the high school band, the color guard, and cheerleaders. Followed by the boy scout and girl scout troops, the veteran's post had a small float and the local equestrian barn decorated their horses and joined the fun. Liv's favorite was the local kids and their bikes.

Bella used to love to decorate her bike in red, white, and blue, weaving streamers between the spokes and tying pom-poms to the handlebars. She'd ride her way through town with friends and neighbors cheering her on from the sidewalks. Liv would stock her bike basket full of Hubba Bubba gum to pass out to parade-goers. Michael had always ridden right alongside his daughter while Liv packed nearly the same parade picnic every year and watched from the front of Beyond Blooms, meeting them in the exact same spot she sat now for snacks and cocktails.

Liv and her friends gathered together on the grassy crest of the hill that looked out over the marina and the lake beyond. The sun, just beginning to set, gave off the wonderful lavender glow of evening. Time stretched wide and long as they waited for dusk to settle completely and the fireworks to start. There was a low buzz of energy, a rumbling of voices melded together as the excitement of summer settled around the friends. Liv smiled and waved to people she knew—which were a lot considering she'd lived in this little town nearly her entire life and so had Michael. She also waved to some she didn't know, just a handful, who had recognition in their eyes. *Her readers.* She tried her best to smile and wave, knowing they were wondering.

"Hey, Mom, Hannah just texted me. She's down by the dock with some friends. I'm going to head down there and say hi," Bella said.

"Oh … okay. It's getting close to time, hun. Make sure you make your way back in a little while. I don't want to be looking for you in the dark."

"One, I managed to keep myself alive for the last nine months without you telling me when it got dark out. Two, we have these little things in our pockets called phones. It's literally impossible to lose me. Particularly since you have been tracking me since I was fifteen years—"

"You talkin' to your momma like that, darlin'?"

"Frannie!" Bella screamed in delight.

"How did ya guess?" Frannie laughed as she came up behind Bella and scooped her up in a hug. Liv smiled as her friends loved on her daughter, even as Bella's behavior stung.

"I was hoping you'd get here before I left! Took you long enough! What could be more important than coming to see me?" She smiled as Frannie gave Bella one last snug around her shoulders. "Did I hear you say y'all leaving already?" Frannie asked.

"Just me. I'm going to meet some friends."

"Be good, darlin'. You hear?"

"I hear you, I hear you." Bella kissed Frannie on the cheek, hugged Lucy and Maggie, and waved goodbye to her mom before stopping to hand out high-fives to Cash and Carson.

Frannie smiled at her friend's daughter as she walked away and turned toward Liv. "She went away last fall sweet as pie and came back with all the answers, didn't she?"

"Yes. She certainly did. I knew she'd come home more independent. I just didn't know she'd come home full of so much sass. She's been a pill the last couple days. Actually, I think maybe I just forgot what a pill she was before she left. The whole 'absence makes the heart grow fonder' thing?" Liv attempted a laugh.

"I am sure exams were really hard and she's tired," Maggie added, her eyes cutting away from Liv's when they met over Liv's pitcher and Maggie's empty drink. It wasn't unusual for Maggie to defend Bella when Liv was frustrated. Maggie was empathetic to a fault and always saw the other person's point of view. But not particularly when Bella was, in fact, being a brat. The slight registered to Liv, although she wasn't sure how to interpret it.

"Hey don't look now, but Angela is at three o'clock." Maggie pasted her customer-service smile on her face as the bleach blonde walked straight for them.

"Well, look who's here," Angela said. Her smile dripped syrup sweet, and her eyes were full to the brim with sarcasm. Looking at her now, Liv was reminded that what she lacked in personality and morals she made up for in beauty. Angela was gorgeous. Tall, slim, blonde hair. Her nose just big enough to make her interesting and her chin just small enough to offset the attitude. She was the perfect villain. Maybe Liv should incorporate an Angelaesque character into her next book?

"Hey, Angela," Lucy answered first, her smile as big and as fake as she could make it. There wasn't much Angela wouldn't do to get under Lucy's skin. They were, essentially, the only two real estate shows in town. Even though there was enough inventory for both women to be successful, they both preferred to own it all. And Angela didn't always manage her business dealings with a lot of scruples. Lucy had lost a few deals over the years to her rival because she simply refused to play dirty.

"I wanted to introduce you to my friend Josh."

Liv, standing behind the row of chairs, continued to ignore Angela and her guest by busing herself with organizing the picnic basket and cooler after Carson and Cash had ransacked it. She didn't have much use for Angela, and frankly didn't care if Angela thought she was rude.

"Josh? Nice to meet you. I'm Lucy Nash." Lucy smiled.

"Hi there, Lucy. Josh Hart."

Liv startled, stopping what she was doing, and listened again as she watched from the corner of her eye as Lucy and Josh shook hands.

Could it be?

"Have we met before? You look awfully familiar," Maggie asked, rising out of her chair and coming to greet Josh.

"I think we may have." His deep, slow-paced voice reached Liv's heart like a lightning bolt. "I spent a few summers here as a teenager with my parents. We own the old Chandler Cottage just north of town."

"Oh yes! I remember now. Your parents had a boat down on the docks, didn't they? Hey, Liv?" Maggie asked as she turned to her oldest friend. "Do you remember Josh?"

Liv turned and offered her hand to Josh quietly, hoping neither Maggie nor Josh would notice her shaking. He squeezed his warm fingers around her much smaller ones, clasping both his hands around hers. Suddenly she was staring into a pair of piercing, very familiar, blue eyes. Before she could answer, Josh spoke.

"Liv Harrison. I've always wondered what happened to you."

Chapter 7

"It's Liv Pennington, now," Angela answered with an undeniable emphasis on the fact that Liv's last name was not what it was.

"Of course. Liv Harrison is circa 1988? Sophomore year?" Josh smiled and nodded, his head tilting just slightly to the right. His eyes, locked and loaded on Liv, were as bright and blue as she remembered. Of course, he'd aged in other ways. A few wrinkles showcased his eyes when he smiled. His hair, although largely still blonde, was threaded with touches of silver. Still handsome.

"Oh yes, I think it was sophomore year. Well, the summer between sophomore year and junior year," Liv answered, realizing too late that she had offered up far too much detail to continue to feign vague recollection of the man standing in front of her. Liv fought to keep her hands from tucking her hair behind her ears—her telltale sign of nerves. The ladies would certainly recognize that. It really didn't matter—her cheeks were burning red, giving her away. Of course, she could always blame that on a hot flash.

The truth was, she more than recognized him. She remembered him. Well.

"How *funny* that you two would know each other! The world really is a small place, isn't it?" Angela added, stringing her long, thin arm through Josh's. Josh, for his part, continued looking at Liv.

Liv took a step back, away from Josh and Angela. "It is a small world," Liv added, nodding her head.

"I can't believe this little town *still* has the Kickoff to Summer Festival! I loved it when I was here and I am really enjoying it tonight, too. Living near Detroit, it's so nice to see a small town keep its … small-townness? Is that a word?" Josh laughed at himself.

"You know, I totally agree," Angela said. Saccharine sweet and one hundred percent lying. "There is a small faction of people that want to get rid of the parade and fireworks. They would prefer a more upscale event. But I, for one, am all about keeping traditions. Families and people are the backbone of our communities. Which is what makes Blue Water Bay such an inviting, wonderful place to live."

"You don't have to sell him a house, Angie. He already owns one." Lucy smirked back. Maggie and Liv looked at each other and giggled silently. Liv's shoulders shrugged as she smiled back. Angela had been the head of the committee that started the petition to replace the parade and fireworks with a plated charity dinner. It had gotten zero traction—in fact the committee included only Angela and her assistant Monica.

"Yes, it really was a shame how some of y'all were trying to dismantle the festival. It's such a nice start to summer and—" Before Frannie could finish, there was a loud crash behind her.

"Cash! I'm going to get you!" Carson yelled seconds before Cash came barreling toward the group of adults who were standing awkwardly on the steepest part of the grass hill that rolled down toward the amphitheater.

"Boys! No!" Maggie, adept at jumping out of the way of her rambunctious boys, slid seamlessly out of the line of fire as she yelled for the twins to stop. Lucy held her spiked lemonade high in the air to avoid spilling and stepped backward out of the way. Frannie reached out an arm to lasso Cash—or was it Carson?—but missed.

And before she knew what happened, Liv, propelled forward by the full force of a tag-avoiding ten-year-old boy running into her back, landed squarely in-between Josh's open arms. Beside her, Angela went flying in the second round of attack—straight backward—as Carson came bursting after his brother. She landed on her back end, streaking her white jeans in fierce, green grass stains, and somehow a well-placed glass of spiked lemonade landed right on top of Angela's long, fake, blonde hair.

"Heathens," Lucy murmured under her breath, barely able to contain a smile.

"I'm—I'm so sorry, Angela," Maggie sputtered out, trying to look sincere.

"I can't even. What just happened?" Angela murmured as she pulled sticky, wet, blonde clumps of hair off of her face. Looking up, she saw Josh, his arms wrapped around Olivia, and asked, "Josh, could you take me home? I am suddenly not in the mood for the fireworks."

"Of course. Let's get you back to your car," he answered. A smile, directed toward Liv, turned up just enough to create a sexy, side-ways grin that said he somehow understood the inherent justice of what just happened. Still holding Liv steady with his hands on her arms, he squeezed both of her tiny elbows as he made sure she was steady on her feet. Their bodies nearly touching, just inches away, Liv could hear him breathing. She could smell the subtle scent of sandalwood? Bergamot? Tobacco? She wasn't sure what, only that he smelled decidedly wonderful and decidedly ... male. Her body simmered. It had been a long time since she had been this close to a man, and decades since she'd been this close to *this* man.

Clenching her stomach in an effort to pull herself together, Liv took a step back, out of Josh's arms and back into her own lonely space.

"I have a few napkins. Would that help, Angela?" she offered.

"No. No, I don't need anybody's napkins. I'm fine," she insisted as she pulled herself to standing with belated help from Josh. As she stood up, unfolding what felt like miles of legs and arms, Liv watched as Angela clenched Josh's hand for support and didn't let go. "Can we go? I am .... sticky. And cold."

"Yes, of course. Well, it was nice to meet everyone, or see you again as the case may be. I am sure I'll see you around." Josh smiled at the group and turned his blue eyes toward Liv. "It was really nice seeing you, Liv." And with that, Josh—the sandy-haired boy who had turned her world upside down one summer thirty years ago—turned and walked away, again.

Chapter 8

Liv and Lucy walked toward the center of town after the fireworks, having first stopped at the Blue Moon Ice Cream Company for cones. Frannie had already headed to the beer tent down at the yacht club to save a table. Maggie had long since dragged her heathens home. Lucy was escorting Liv up from the marina and through town before heading back to join Frannie and listen to the band.

"Are you sure you don't want to join us at the beer tent? I hear the band is good tonight. That eighties cover band you love." Lucy's voice sprang upward as she pleaded with Liv to join them.

"No, I want to be back if Bella changes her mind and decides to come home." Liv had gotten a text from Bella before the fireworks even began that she had hooked up with Hannah and would be staying the night at her house. Liv was pleased that Bella and Hannah had apparently made up. She hadn't gotten a chance to ask Bella what happened between the two—

and now it seemed she didn't need to. Still, she couldn't help feeling disappointed. Sure, she knew her daughter was just home from college and that meant a different level of independence and freedom. Liv had just been hoping to spend some time with her, and that hadn't happened yet. She took a deep breath and reminded herself to be patient.

"Are you sure?" Lucy asked again.

"I'm sure." Liv licked around the outside edge of her ice cream, trying to contain the drips. She slung her picnic basket up around her elbow to free up her hands so she could rearrange her napkin around the cone—and changed the subject. "I know Maggie was embarrassed, but I don't think I've ever seen justice being served more accurately than when Cash and Carson crashed into Angela."

Lucy laughed through swallowing a bite of her coconut chocolate chip. "Did you see her face? And what is up with carrying on about the committee to replace the parade and fireworks? It was her thing! Her petition! What a snake she is."

"It was pretty ironic. It wasn't five seconds after she lied that she got plowed over. That's better than Pinocchio's nose growing!"

"When she went flying, I nearly spilled my drink—I didn't. But I almost did. The whole situation didn't turn out so bad for you, either." Lucy's voice lilted up into a smile as she used her shoulder to bump Olivia as they walked, trying to get her attention. "Liv Harrison."

Olivia continued to lick her ice cream cone, readjusting the napkin again as she feigned managing a melting ice cream mess that wasn't happening. She was thankful for the dark—the last thing she needed was for Lucy to see her smoldering red cheeks again.

"Poor Maggie. Those boys are a handful and Bruce needs to—"

"So—wait a minute," Lucy interrupted Olivia's attempt to change the subject. "Let me get this right. I can't believe you knew that handsome specimen of a man when we were kids and *I* never heard about him?"

Liv laughed and hoped Lucy didn't hear the hint of nerves that edged out the comfort of her voice. "He was a summer kid. I didn't know him well. I think he was here the summer you went to work on Mackinac Island. Remember? Maggie was working at the golf course, and I was at the dock. He spent a lot of time on his parents' boat so I knew him from the marina. Filled up their boat a couple of times."

"Ahhhh ..." Lucy looked at Liv, having figured out a piece of the puzzle. "If memory serves, that was the summer Michael was in London?"

"I think it may have been? I don't remember, exactly," Liv hedged.

"And he's *always wondered what happened to you,* Liv? He had no trouble remembering you. It had to be more than you working at the dock and him hanging on his parents' boat. Come on, give me the skinny!"

"There isn't any to give," Olivia answered.

"Of all the summers for me to *not* be in town! He's beautiful!"

"He's handsome, I guess," Liv answered.

"You guess? You *guess?* Liv. Your husband is dead. You are not. It's okay for you to think a man is handsome. A *single* man in this case."

"Single? How do you know he's single?"

"Are you questioning me, Olivia Pennington? I have dated more men than you, Frannie, and Maggie all put together. He's single. Trust me."

"Well, I'm not."

Lucy draped her arm around Liv's shoulders. "Nobody said anything about you, Liv. Although …"

"Luce. Stop right there. I'm not up for it. Not even up for thinking about it. I have too much on my plate to entertain even the slightest notion of dating again. And have you noticed my daughter is a handful right now? I don't have the interest, time, or energy. Besides, I had the best. There is nowhere to go but down. And

I'm not interested in that." Liv had repeated this message any number of times in answer to any suggestion by her friends that she get back out there. Start living again. Maybe go on a few dates. She had to hand it to them, they didn't give up. But none of them understood.

"Michael was the best. He was." Lucy knew her friend and she knew when she'd been beaten. "You okay to walk home alone? Maybe we should call you an Uber?" The house was south of town. She could follow the sidewalk nearly all the way there, and the path was lit with street lamps.

"There is *no* reason to call an Uber. I'm fine. I'm used to being alone."

Lucy kissed Liv on the cheek. "I love you, Liv. Text me when you get home?"

The two friends parted ways, Lucy heading for the bright lights and loud noises of the band and beer tent, and Liv headed for her quiet house in the woods perched on the edge of the bluff keeping watch over the lake.

Chapter 9

Liv finished her cone and threw the napkin in a trash bin as she walked along the sidewalk path that would take her home. Her hands now free, she pulled the picnic basket up over her shoulder. The wind had picked up just a touch since the fireworks had ended—they had nearly missed a small squall earlier in the evening and she wondered now if another was preparing to land.

Within a block of downtown, when the lights dimmed to only a street lamp now and then, the rain began to sprinkle. Just a bit at first, enough that Liv laughed and quickened her footsteps. Within seconds, it had turned into an all-out downpour. She considered putting down her picnic basket and making a run for it, but it was her favorite—she'd used it for years. In fact, it was one of the first things she bought herself after her first book was published.

Michael had laughed. "A picnic basket? That's what you want?" Her feelings hadn't been hurt; he thought she should buy something more extravagant. But Liv was then—and still was now—a romantic. She wanted an old-style, wicker picnic basket with flaps opening on each side. One that she could pack for date nights, or picnics with friends. She hiked the basket up higher on her shoulder, attempting to make it easier to move quickly. She couldn't leave the basket. The rain would ruin it, or it would be taken. She'd just have to continue putting one foot in front of the other and slop her way through the rain and puddles.

She'd made this trek from town hundreds if not thousands of times before. In fact, this sidewalk path was the beginning of one of her favorite running routes. She'd walked and ran it at all times of day and night, alone and in groups. So she wasn't surprised when the lights of a car panned the path in front of her from behind. She was, however, concerned at first that the car couldn't see her. They seemed to be veering in her direction just a bit. Her heart rate sped up, and so did her footsteps. Blue Water Bay was a nice town, and crime was nearly non-existent, so Liv wasn't *really* worried. But also, she was a writer—well, used to be a writer—and her imagination could be considered "overactive" at best, even in real life. She picked up her pace to a slow jog to move her feet quickly toward home.

"Liv!" a voice shouted. "Olivia!" Hearing her name, she stopped and turned around. She didn't have far to go, but a ride would be heaven-sent. The voice sounded familiar, although she couldn't place it immediately. But Blue Water Bay was full of people she knew and not many that she didn't. Liv approached the passenger window, putting some distance between the driver and herself, just as the window rolled down.

Josh.

"Hey, get in! I'll give you a ride."

Surprised, Olivia stuttered out, "Oh, no. No. That's okay. Thanks," before she turned and walked away.

Her small legs were no match for the car, and Josh rolled up next to her again. "Don't be ridiculous. Get in the car and let me take you home. It's dark. I barely saw you with all this rain. I can't leave you out here to get hit by a drunk guy leaving the beer tent."

That did it. She didn't need Bella being an orphan. Liv turned and walked quickly back toward the passenger door and jumped into the car. Once settled, with her picnic basket on her lap, she stared forward. Her reflection glared back at her in the windshield. She was soaked, her mascara running, and her white shirt clung to her like Saran Wrap. Self-consciousness crept up from her belly until she readjusted the shirt away from her tiny chest. Her eyes slid sideways toward Josh, who was carefully looking behind him, waiting for enough space to merge back onto the road. Obviously, the rain had driven most of the beer-tent-goers home. The traffic was unusually heavy.

"Thanks. I'm sorry, I'm getting your car soaked."

"It's all right. It's a rental. Mine's in the shop." Josh smiled back over his shoulder as he waited for a few more cars to pass. Liv smiled in his direction, and they sat there in silence. Her hands were clasped together, sitting on top of her picnic basket.

"Why don't you put that in the back seat, give yourself some room. This isn't the biggest car I've ever seen," Josh suggested.

Not wanting to give up the cover the basket gave her, but realizing she was squished and it may be more awkward to refuse, Liv lifted the basket and put it in the back seat. Suddenly, she felt closer to Josh. As if she'd shifted herself over into the middle seat of a truck. Her cheeks flushed. *Again?* She must be having a hot flash. Which wasn't terrible, because frankly she'd gotten a little cold in the rain.

"Where to? I assume you don't live at your parents' house anymore?"

Liv laughed despite being uncomfortable. "No, I guess not. Straight ahead."

Josh waited until he could pull out into traffic easily,

and they traveled in silence for a few minutes. Liv put her hand on her heart. Her cheeks were flushed, and now her heart was racing. The beat pulsed loudly from her chest to her ears, making it hard to concentrate. Although, she wasn't sure what she was supposed *to* concentrate on—only that she shouldn't be concentrating on Josh. Which she was finding difficult.

"So, this is strange, isn't it?" Josh asked, his face lighting up briefly with the headlights of a passing car. It was then, with a flash of light across his features, that Liv saw him. Young Josh. Josh circa 1988. Somewhere in the profile of this stranger sitting next to her, Liv saw the young man she knew. She recognized the cleft in his chin, blending smoothly with a strong jawline and well-set cheekbones. Long lashes decorated his bright blue eyes. The flush in her cheeks deepened.

"It's unexpected, that's for sure." Liv smiled carefully. "How long are you here for?" she added, not wanting to sit in awkward silence but also finding she was curious.

"I'm not sure. I've just finished a big project at work and am taking some time off. I own my own consulting company—Hart Consulting. I work in the manufacturing and automotive industry, like everybody else in Detroit." Josh smiled. "My dad passed away a few years ago, and my mom has done quite well until the last six months or so. I'm going to stay a few weeks, enjoy the boat and the lake, and get a better picture of how my mom really is."

"That's too bad," Liv answered and then added, "That your mom isn't doing well, not that you're going to enjoy the boat and the lake." *Stop talking, Liv,* she told herself.

"I'm not completely sure what's going on. She has been getting confused on the phone a little and she's lost weight. It's just me; my brother died a few years before my dad."

Liv clasped her hands together. She hadn't really known Josh's brother; she'd only met him a few times. He'd been older—quite a bit, if she remembered correctly. Still, he would have been young when he passed. Just like Michael.

Liv offered sympathies again, and Josh simply smiled. Liv understood. People didn't know what to say when you told them you'd lost someone you loved. And the reality was, something was usually better than nothing. Because in the end none of it made the ache go away.

Josh's mother had been a beauty when they were young. Raven dark hair, cupid's bow lips, and the moxie to wear a bikini to the beach when all the other mothers stuck to one-pieces to cover up their cesarean scars and stretch marks. Liv had liked and admired her back then.

"So, is Angela helping you sell the house or something?" she asked.

Josh laughed. "Well, I think that's her angle. But I don't have any plans to do so, yet."

Liv nodded—she understood completely.

"Is your husband home?" Josh asked, tipping his head toward her wedding ring. Liv considered the question. Was he coming on to her? Or just making small talk with an old friend? It had been so long since Liv had dated—and even longer since she'd been in this close of proximity to a man that wasn't Michael—she couldn't tell. In fact, Liv realized the last time she sat shotgun in a car with a man other than Michael was the last time she rode shotgun with Josh Hart.

"Oh …" Liv looked at her ring. The benefit to a widow living in the town she grew up in was that there were not a lot—if any—occasions where Liv had been forced to announce (or explain) Michael's death. Had she lived in a big city, or traveled much since she lost him, she may have been ready with a canned statement. As it was, she was unprepared. So she stuck with the simple truth. "My husband passed away unexpectedly."

Josh hesitated for a moment and took a deep breath before speaking.

"I'm sorry, Liv. That's terrible." He took his eyes from the road briefly to look in her direction. For a second, Liv was afraid he would reach for her hand in sympathy. He didn't, and that left Liv feeling softly disappointed.

"Two years ago earlier this month, actually. We're the first driveway after the crossroad up ahead." Liv pointed toward her mailbox, indicating her drive.

"Got it." Josh was quiet, his blinker clicking as they waited to pull into Liv's long driveway.

"Thanks for the ride, Josh," Liv said as they rounded the turn and drove toward the house. "I really do appreciate it. And again, I'm sorry for getting your car all wet."

"Hey, it's no problem at all, Liv. I really have wondered about you over the years. I'd always hoped you were well." Josh smiled, and Liv felt her heart quicken again. Even with his quick glance in her direction, his eyes seemed to bore into hers, as if he was searching for the echo of the girl he used to know.

Josh's car rolled to a stop, his headlights shining directly on the side porch. Liv pulled her eyes together in an effort to see more clearly through the windshield and the rain. Josh followed her gaze.

"Is something wrong?" Josh asked.

"I'm not sure …" Liv leaned even closer as she

reached for the door handle. Her heart had gone from a quick beat to a race of fear. She didn't want to be right, but her mind couldn't make any other sense of what she saw: a body slumped by the back door.

Chapter 10

"Oh my God!" Liv yelled. "Bella! Bella!" Liv ripped open the car door, leaving it ajar behind her as she ran toward the porch. It had taken Liv just a second once she realized it was, in fact, a body slumped on her porch for her to realize that body was Bella. Fear spread like hot lava across her chest and into her arms as her feet splashed through puddles on the nearly century-old stone walkway.

"Bella! Bella!" Liv screamed at the body slumped on the porch steps. Her fingers were numb and tingling by the time she reached her daughter. She could barely catch her breath and hadn't realized that Josh had gotten to Bella first. This couldn't be happening again. Memories of Michael dead on the floor flooded Liv's mind. Looking at her daughter piled up against the back door—the two visions combined inexplicably. *Michael-Bella-Michael-Bella*. This couldn't happen to her again. She simply couldn't bear it.

"Bella! Honey!" Liv put her hands on either side of

Bella's cheeks to tip her face forward as Josh held her up. Bella moaned when they moved her, taking in a breath of air. Relief flooded Liv as quickly as tears fell from her eyes.

"Oh my God. She smells like a tequila distillery. Bella, honey, wake up!"

Liv tapped her daughter's face lightly. And just like that, with rain pouring down around the unlikely trio, Bella's eyes opened. What had looked like utter tragedy had been her daughter, sleeping off a night of too many tequila shots.

"Hey, Mom," Bella said quietly, her words smushing together. She looked around, her eyes vacant. "I forgot my key … or I lost it? I don't 'member." Her eyes faded back to closed.

Without a second's hesitation, Josh scooped Bella up, one arm under her knees and another around her shoulders. "Open the door, Liv." He nodded his head in the direction of the screen door.

Reveling in a strange pool of lingering fear, embarrassment, and pure fury, Liv did as she was asked. It had been two long years of making all the decisions by herself: college, scholarships, bills, taxes, dinner. The simple act of having Josh there to help navigate what to do brought a flood of relief. The sensation spread her heart wide in her chest, giving her space to breathe that she hadn't had in quite some time. The relief was as thoroughly soaking as the storm outside and it felt euphoric. So much so, guilt tinged the outside of her mind. How could she be relieved at a moment like this?

Josh walked with Bella through the side door, past the kitchen, and into the living room. Liv guided him along the way, throwing the pile of pillows she had staged on the couch onto the floor just before he laid Bella down. As Josh pulled off Bella's shoes, Liv quickly stopped in the bathroom for a few towels and a trash can for Bella in case she was ill.

Bella roused once she was lying down. Looking up at Josh, her eyes squinted, trying to make sense of what was happening.

"Who are you?" Bella asked, her tone neither pleasant nor confrontational, which was a certain sign of the amount of tequila she'd consumed. Liv had no doubt that if she were in her right mind, Bella would be angry at the intrusion of a strange man in her father's house.

"I am an old friend of your mom's who just happened to be in the right place at the right time tonight." Josh pulled his lips together in a small smile, straightening up to his full height and squeezing his shoulders back in a stretch.

"Hmm ... mmhmm," Bella agreed with Josh and rolled toward the inside of the couch. Liv busied herself with wiping her daughter off with towels, although she wasn't nearly as wet as the two adults.

"She must have gotten home before it started to rain. At least she passed out under the roof of the porch. It must have protected her. Thank God something did." Liv handed Josh a towel.

"Thanks," he answered as he dried his face and hair. Liv watched as he pulled the towel over his closed eyes. She tried to draw her attention away—it seemed too intimate of an act to watch—but she couldn't.

"No, thank you. I'm really sorry. She's never done anything like this before. Ever."

"First summer home after freshman year in college?"

"Yes, how'd you guess?"

"I have twins. They just finished up their junior year—one at a small private school in Virginia and another at Ohio State. Freshman year is hard on them. Coming home can be, too."

"Yes, I suppose so. I've just never had this kind of trouble with her before. I mean sure, she's full of sass. But this …" Liv looked down at Bella, who seemed to be peacefully sleeping. Her breathing was even and comfortable. "I *cannot* believe she did this."

"Don't be too hard on her. Sounds like she's had a hard last couple of years." Josh's lips turned up gently on the corners.

Liv took a deep gulp of air. "No. It hasn't been easy," Liv admitted.

"Plus, teenagers aren't known to make the best decisions. I seem to remember you and I making our fair share of questionable choices." Josh used his hands to fold the damp towel in his hands before crossing his arms against his chest in a comfortable, familiar gesture.

Liv wanted to answer, to say something witty. To laugh about their teenage summer romance. But all she could do was look in those bright blue eyes for a second before turning away.

Josh responded, "Listen, I better get going."

"Oh, of course, yes. Of course. Thank you, again. So much. I don't know how I would have gotten her inside without you."

"My guess is you would have been fine. I think the father in me overreacted. She's drunk, obviously, but she would have made it inside."

"Either way. Thank you for the ride and for the help. I won't lie and pretend like I'm not embarrassed—"

"Hey, absolutely not. We all make mistakes. She'll learn from it. Like I said, don't be too hard on her. Maybe this is an opportunity for you two to talk. She'll feel bad enough in the morning as it is."

"You are probably right." Liv sighed. "Oh my goodness. Parenting isn't for the weak, is it?"

"Ha! No, no it's not." Josh smiled again, and this time Liv did too. "Maybe I'll see you around?" he asked.

"I do live here," Liv blurted out. She'd intended to be funny, but once the words were out of her mouth, they sounded … inviting? Liv's cheeks began to burn that deep, crimson red (again) as embarrassment settled around her.

Josh leaned forward and reached for her arm, touching it ever so lightly before kissing her on the cheek. His voice was low and soft when he said, "Well then, I know where to find you."

Chapter 11

Liv Harrison. *Pennington,* he reminded himself. After all these years of wondering what had happened to the pixie-small, sweet soul of a girl he'd fallen for—hard—the summer after his freshman year in college, he finally knew. She'd never left Blue Water Bay. Of course, it had occurred to him over the years to look for her here. It wasn't like he'd never been back. He'd visited his parents a couple times each summer when they were in residence at their cottage. Looking back, he found it amazing that he hadn't run into her until now.

Ironically, he had Angela to thank for that. *Angela.* Angela and Justin, Josh's older brother, had been involved. The last time he'd seen her had been at his brother's funeral. Josh cringed as he remembered the pretty blonde on the ground with lemonade—which was spiked by the smell of it—pouring down her face. Poor Angela.

They'd actually had a good time together, catching up until they ran into Olivia and her friends. Angela had gotten instantly possessive—holding his hand and dropping her arms around his waist. He was no stranger to women's attention. Being a tall, successful, unattached man in Detroit meant there were plenty of dates to choose from. But Angela's attention had given him the distinct impression he was being used. He wasn't sure how or why, and frankly he wasn't all that bothered by it. Walking back, she'd dropped the act and seemed genuinely embarrassed, and more than a little irritated. He was glad he'd escorted her back to her car, but that was as far as that would go. The only feeling that lingered after he'd seen Angela was sadness. He missed his brother.

Justin had been Josh's best friend and business partner. In fact, he'd been the reason Josh had the capital to even start Hart Consulting. Josh had been the brains, and Justin—eight years his senior—had been the cash. Justin had gotten in early and came out big with the tech boom. He'd used his profits to help Josh get started, keeping his hands out of the business end and letting Josh run the day-to-day operations how he saw fit.

There were days Josh forgot Justin was gone. Like when he watched Justin's favorite football team, The Green Bay Packers lose and he reached to pick up the phone to give him a hard time. Moments like that took his breath away. The small, in-between moments. The moments that looked like nothing, but in fact were everything.

Justin had been larger than life. A smidge over six foot two—and just a shade taller than Josh—his booming voice and contagious laughter always dominated a room. He'd been the picture of health: fit, trim, handsome. In fact, the day before he'd gone to the doctor for back pain, Justin had played thirty-six holes of golf with Josh and their father. Six weeks later, he was gone. The cancer had moved so quickly, Josh barely had time to process the diagnosis before his brother was gone.

Their father died just a few years later. Losing their oldest son had been exquisitely hard on his parents. His father never recovered, and Josh was certain he would have lived longer if Justin had. But his mother had an inherent strength that Josh admired and drew from. She was a beautiful woman, even in these later years. Perhaps especially. But it was her strength that drew people to her. Of course, he'd asked his mother to join him at the Kickoff to Summer party, but she hadn't been up to it. Another red flag to Josh that Dorothy wasn't quite herself. His mom would have never passed up the opportunity to socialize in town.

Josh took a deep breath as he connected a hose to the water spigot at the end of the dock. His parents' boat had been in storage for several years, his mom refusing to sell. She'd had it serviced twice a year and had kept her dock space in the town marina. It seemed to be an unneeded expense, but after losing her son and then her husband in short order, Josh wasn't about to insist she give anything up she didn't want to.

So, one of the first things he did when he got to Blue Water Bay was pull the boat out of its dry dock storage and get it in the water. Today he was giving the old girl a good cleaning. The sun was out, it was getting warmer by the minute, and Josh was ready to get to work. There was nothing quite like manual labor to allow a man to think. His mind could wander without a guardian. Which is what Josh needed—time to think. He smiled and tipped his face up toward the sun. His eyes closed as he let the sun drip down over his shoulders.

Getting to work, his mind went immediately to worries about his mother. He'd suspected his mom's memory was fading. She'd gotten confused a few times during their frequent telephone calls and sometimes told the same story twice. But being here in Blue Water Bay with her, in person, it was harder for her to camouflage how much she'd declined. It was a difficult thing to witness, and there were plenty of decisions that needed to be made.

Summer Love

Just thinking about everything that had to be done—the work on the house, the boat—threatened to overwhelm him. He still had to run his company. His right-hand man, Grant, would look after things while he was out, but he couldn't play hooky forever. Josh took a deep sigh as he contemplated what to do.

And most importantly, he had his twins—Lacy and Zane—to keep tabs on. Granted, college juniors didn't take much time, but still Josh liked to stay in touch, to be included in their lives.

Since his divorce, the role he played had changed. Dina and Josh had divorced when the kids were in middle school. Just when it gets difficult. Not the kind of difficult that having twin toddlers was, but the kind of difficult that happens when your kids have to start making decisions that can affect their entire lives. He'd tried as hard as he could to be there for his kids while still maintaining his business.

He'd not missed a sporting event—ju-jitsu and tennis for Lacy, football and baseball for Zane. He'd not missed a parent-teacher conference. He would have preferred to be there daily, to be there when they went off to school and eat dinner together every night. Not that he necessarily wanted to stay married—to be honest, he was happy enough, but Dina had been right. Well, right in that she knew they weren't as happy as they could be.

Josh wasn't sure Dina had traded their mediocre happiness for any great love—but when someone evaluates future partners based on bank accounts rather than compatibility, it gets a little difficult. Still, he didn't harbor any ill will for Dina. If anything, he'd made peace with the whole thing.

The boat was in fairly good shape for a vessel that hadn't seen the water in several years. He started down below in the cabin, organizing cupboards and taking inventory of what he would need to stock. The monotony of the task was comforting. With his mom's memory beginning to fail and his brother and father gone, he felt a strange sense of ownership, and urgency, to preserve their family legacy. He wasn't sure what that looked like yet, or what he could even do. All he knew was life was lonely without them. Which is why he was here, in Blue Water Bay.

Oliva's face popped into his mind as he worked, scrubbing the deck and wiping down the vinyl of the seats. Not the Olivia that he knew when he was a teenager. No, the Olivia he saw at the festival. The one whose eyes were soft with sadness.

The summer they had spent together, her own parents had divorced. Josh and Liv had spent a lot of time talking through that. Dorothy had also given the young

Summer Love

Olivia some advice and extra special care during those months. In a lot of ways, watching Olivia go through her parents splitting up had given Josh a guide for his own separation and divorce. Years before he'd even be married, Olivia had given him a window into what his children would go through when his marriage fell apart. The gift came years after their relationship ended, but Josh was always grateful for that.

Josh wasn't one for dramatics or overthinking. But his thoughts returned to the question of why, after all this time, had he run into Olivia? Josh still found his heart beat faster at the sight of Olivia. Her small features and tiny stature evoked the caveman in him. Just like that summer, he felt drawn to protect her.

Which seems funny thinking about it now. She'd survived all this time without him, even made it through the devastating loss of her husband. Still, his tender urge to protect her, keep her from harm, was as strong as it had been in 1988. It didn't help that she'd literally been shoved into his arms by a rogue ten-year-old. Feeling her body pressed against his re-ignited a flame that had smoldered for decades.

Josh smiled and sat back on his heels, taking a break from scrubbing the deck on his knees. He got up and hosed down the corner he'd been cleaning.

Harmony Beach.

Images of the last night he and Liv spent together flooded his memory. A beach fire. The stars. He shook his head. It hadn't been the first time he'd relived that night, but now, after touching her again, the memories were vivid.

He'd wondered how long it had been since her husband had passed. It would be easy to jump down a Google rabbit hole and come up with an answer, but he wasn't going to do that. Anything he knew about her husband, he wanted to know from her. Of course, this was a small town and he was likely to run into her again. He was certain their paths would cross during the course of a small-town summer, even if he was only here a few weeks. Still. He didn't want to take anything for granted.

It occurred to him that maybe he should give her a wide berth, steer clear of her sad eyes. He shook his head again. No, he'd been given the perfect opportunity to see Liv again. And he was going to take it.

Chapter 12

"I hereby call this meetin' of the Ladies of the Round Table to order." Frannie used her best authoritarian voice, which mixed with her still deep southern drawl sounded more like a comedy skit than seriousness.

"Hear, hear!" Liv, Maggie, and Lucy lifted their glasses to toast the lunch with champagne flutes poured to the rim with mimosas. While the ladies had been lifetime friends, it wasn't until Michael died and Maggie, Lucy, and Frannie wanted a reason to *see* Liv on a regular basis did they begin the weekly meetings of the Ladies. It had been Lucy who came up with the name "Ladies of the Round Table," and it had stuck. What had started out as a lifeline for one of them had turned into something none of them could live without.

Each meeting started with one mimosa and sometimes coffee, sometimes more mimosas, followed by brunch and a dissection of the four founding members' current life statuses.

"So, here's a fun one for you. Cash got in trouble in

science class," Maggie said.

"And?" Lucy questioned.

"The teacher was trying to get the class to quiet down and held her hand up like a stop sign. When she said 'stop,' Cash jumped out of his seat and said …"

"No, he did not," Lucy said, starting to laugh and anticipating—correctly—what Cash was about to say. Maggie and Liv waited patiently for the punch line.

"Oh yes he did. He stood up on his chair and sang 'Ice Ice Baby' at the top of his lungs."

When the laughter died down, Liv asked, "Was Carson there, too?"

"Oh goodness, no. They aren't allowed to be in the same classes. The teacher would never make it!" Maggie took a big sip of her mimosa and then put her head in her hand. "I don't know what I am going to do. Honest to goodness, they are such kind, good-hearted boys, but they are *wild*."

"But they come up with the best stories!" Lucy said, still fighting off rolls of laughter. "He's so funny! I bet most of the kids didn't even know what song he was singing!"

Liv, Lucy, and Frannie started laughing again, big gulping waves of laughter. Tiny tears slipped out of Liv's eyes as she squeezed them tight, trying to catch her breath as she laughed.

Summer Love

"It's *not* funny!" Maggie insisted as she herself melted into a puddle of giggles.

"You will survive, Maggie, I promise. If anybody can do it, you can! Bella might be a sassy handful, but that story takes the cake!" Liv hugged Maggie.

Before the silliness died down, Misty came by with a second round of mimosas. She was average in height and stature with thick, silver hair—cut in a cute bob. Her round, rosy cheeks gave her the sweet aura of a grandma. And the ever-mischievous sparkle in her eyes reminded you she was still very much a force to be reckoned with. Misty's husband, Dutch, had passed away a few years before Michael. Misty had saved special words of advice, casseroles, and gently placed bouquets of flowers especially for Liv in the first year after Michael died. The two women had fostered a quiet, kindred relationship that Liv both relied on and appreciated.

"This is looking like a two-bottle brunch to me, ladies." She smiled, topping off glasses and setting down both the champagne bottle and a carafe of orange juice.

"We don't need much juice, Mist!" Lucy said, having been the one to recover the quickest from her laughing spell. "I actually prefer just sitting the orange juice *next* to the champagne instead of actually mixing them together."

"Well, isn't that how everyone does it?" Misty smiled, her lips turning up on the left side. "You all seem to be having a good time this morning!"

Lucy filled Misty in on Cash's budding musical career, and the laughter started all over again.

"Oh Maggie, I know it's exhausting now. But trust me. That quick wit and energy will take them far."

"If I can keep them alive that long!" Maggie lamented.

"You know my Ryan, he was a handful. There were days I told Dutch, if I make it to the end of the day and we are both still alive, I did my job." Misty smiled and reached down and squeezed Olivia's wrist. Liv tapped her friend's hand as Misty returned to the counter to wait on a new round of customers.

"How is Bella?" Frannie asked.

"Quiet, she's not talking much. Maggie would know better than me. If she's not working at Beyond Blooms, she's in her room." Liv's smile subsided as she reported on her daughter's mood. "I don't know. Something is up but I can't figure out what it is."

Maggie, taking another sip of her mimosa, began to choke.

"You okay, Maggie?" Lucy swiped away Maggie's long blond curls from her back and patted her gently between the shoulder blades.

"Yep, yep. My mimosa just went down funny." Maggie's eyes cast down as she fiddled with a hangnail.

"Did you talk with her about the night of the festival?" Lucy asked. Liv appreciated that even though none of them had ever mothered a daughter, or parented one alone, they were always interested, always invested, and always supportive of Liv and Bella.

"I actually did, but just a little bit. I took Josh's advice and didn't come down hard. I just told her it was dangerous, not to mention illegal. She didn't have much to say. I was hoping by not hounding her about it, she might open up about what's *really* going on. But no luck so far. What about you, Luce? What's up with you?" Liv said, changing the subject. One of the harder parts Liv had found about being a new, or relatively new, widow was that she and her situation were often the focus of everyone's (well-intentioned) attention. At first it felt like a gentle balm on her soul, a quenching of a Sahara dry thirst. Lately, it had taken on a different flavor, almost feeling egotistic to continue to rely on her friends' goodwill without contributing more.

"Same old, same old. Work. CrossFit. And brunch," she added while lifting her mimosa toward her friends and taking the last sip. "How's work for you, Fran?"

Lucy poured the group another round with the bottle Misty had brought.

"Fine. Fine. Nothing exciting. Just working on Olivia's house." Liv nearly laughed out loud. Frannie was *not* good at lying. Frannie would just have to hang on a little longer.

Liv added a smile and a squeeze of her dear friend's knee under the table. Frannie smiled at Liv with pleading eyes. She clearly wanted Liv to take today's meeting to inform their friends of her situation. Instead, she simply said, "She's doing a really nice job at the house, of course."

"So, Liv, Josh's advice?" Lucy asked, changing the subject abruptly—and back to yet another topic Liv didn't want to talk about. *Why had she brought up Josh in the first place?*

Liv felt her cheeks turn crimson red and hoped her friends would assume the champagne had gone straight to her cheeks.

"Well, yeah. Remember I told you he saw me walking in the rain, gave me a ride home, and then helped me get Bella inside when I found my darling daughter drunk on the porch?"

"Mmm hmmm," Luce added. "But I don't remember you mentioning that you had a deep conversation or that he handed out parenting advice?"

"He has two kids, a son and a daughter. Both in college. So, he'd been through this before," Liv continued.

"He suggested I not come down with a sledgehammer, but instead try to get her to open up and talk."

"Sounds like sound advice," Maggie said, slowly taking a sip of her cocktail.

Liv, hot pink cheeks and all, fidgeted in her seat. She hadn't seen Josh since the night of the festival, and for all she knew he was back at work in Detroit—but that didn't mean she hadn't thought about him. Him and his bright blue eyes and long eyelashes. She'd only thought for a moment about his arms wrapped around her when Cash sent her flying. Or maybe two. But those were private thoughts, deep in her mind, she wasn't ready to talk about him with her friends or anybody else. There wasn't even *cause* to talk about him—she wasn't sure why she even brought him up. Other than his name sounded both exciting and comfortable on her lips.

Liv's phone rang, literally saving her by the bell.

"Hey! Y'all know the rule, no answering phone calls at the meetings, Liv!" Frannie chided her friend in good nature.

"Oh gosh, I forgot to turn it on silent," Liv answered as she quickly glanced at the screen before tucking it into her purse. Isla. Again. Her heart began to beat quickly. She was running out of time, and Isla was running out of patience. Liv could see the bridge burning behind her, but felt helpless to put it out. Frannie looked at her and lifted her left eyebrow—a distinctively Frannie gesture—as if she knew *exactly* who called.

Misty delivered their brunch—four slices of quiche Lorraine, four sides of fresh strawberries, and four fresh cups of coffee. Liv laughed and joked with her friends as they finished their meal. The fleeting spike of worry and anxiety she'd felt with Isla's call faded. She could do this. She would go home, right now, and write her heart out.

Yes, she'd left herself in a pretty steep hole, and it would be hard to come up with the kind of daily word count that she would need to hit her deadline, but it wasn't impossible. Yet. She could get this book written, save the house, and avoid telling Bella *and* Lucy and Maggie—and give Frannie a Get Out of Jail Free card by not asking her to keep secrets anymore.

The ladies hugged each other goodbye. Maggie headed next door to work, Lucy to her office, and Frannie—having worked earlier at Liv's house—was headed up to Franklin to check on a specialty tile order. Liv debated stopping in to see Bella before heading home, but decided to take advantage of her growing optimism and hope it translated into words as soon as possible.

Plus, it wasn't likely Bella would be thrilled to see her mom at work. She would continue to take Josh's advice and give her daughter some space.

As she was climbing into her car, Liv dropped her phone out of her purse and onto the sidewalk. "Shoot!" she yelled, scrambling to pick up the device. As she checked the screen for cracks, she saw that a text message from Isla sat unread. Without thinking, Liv clicked on it.

Isla: Liv, you have to call me. Today. Dead serious. Call me.

And just like that, the optimism Liv had felt just minutes before faded to black.

Chapter 13

With noise-canceling headphones, a glass of water, her favorite notebook, best pen, and her phone on airplane mode, Liv sat down. She knew it was unreasonable—and highly unprofessional—to not call Isla back immediately. But she thought if she could just get started, just have a few thousand words going in the right direction, maybe she could bluff Isla long enough to avoid catastrophe.

Pen in hand, she decided to write longhand. Maybe changing the instrument would affect the outcome. She would mind map first—let her mind wander, jot down pieces of ideas, nuggets of inspiration, and see what she could string together for a plot. She'd set herself up a cozy workstation on the front three seasons porch—her office felt too formal, too work-like, to support this different approach and the kitchen hadn't worked so far. The view from here was magnificent and was sure to be inspiring. Not only could she see the water, she could feel the sheer, dramatic drop off of the bluff and smell the pine of the cedar trees surrounding her. Determined, she decided she was not getting up until she had something solid, an idea, a plot, a message—something. Anything.

Bella was at work and would be for several hours, and there was no one or anything to interfere. She looked out the porch window at the water just as a magnificent freighter slowly sailed by. It was far enough in the distance that she couldn't read its name. She'd always wondered what life on a freighter would be like. The ships sailed with skeleton crews, and for as large as they were and the scope of their work, it was fascinating to Liv that such a big machine could operate with so little human support.

What if her main character were the captain of a freighter? A lonely man who had been a tumbleweed his entire life, never setting roots. What if his boat ran aground? Surely it could happen in Lake Huron? What if his boat ran aground and he met a sweet young schoolteacher who lived in the town he washed up in? Liv felt that small flicker, the small light of a fire being lit inside her heart. Right behind it, a bubble of hope.

And then, defeat. She loved the idea, but the research would be extensive—she didn't know anything about freighters. Nothing! She would have to contact shipping yards and talk with captains. The amount of work to just gather the information she needed to write that book with any amount of authenticity would take longer than the time she had left.

She wished Michael was here. He would love this storyline—even though mystery was more of his thing, he would have dove right into researching a freighter captain's life with Liv. He would have had enough knowledge to get her started without researching a thing. A big heaving breath took Liv back to the beginning. Turning the page on her notebook, she left her notes about the captain and the teacher behind.

Michael. My God she missed that man. She missed his presence in the room, she missed hearing his footsteps in the house. She missed the way he loved a beer after dinner and a walk on the beach. She missed the way he knew her, sometimes better than she knew herself. She missed how he would wake in the middle of the night, whisper her name, and pull her to him. She missed having coffee with him in the morning. She missed his help with Bella. She missed how there were pieces of her that only he knew, that their knowledge of each other was exclusive.

She closed her eyes, the headphones canceling out the *drip-drip-drip* of the faucet that Frannie hadn't gotten to yet. Her mind's eye saw the sunrise. *The* Sunrise. Their *Last* Sunrise.

The sky had been brilliant that morning, apricot and peach and lavender and blue. Almost as if the heavens were preparing to celebrate Michael's homecoming. Clouds had hung low, white wisps threaded in between the water and the horizon, making it nearly impossible to tell the difference between Heaven and Earth.

If there were any one moment in their marriage she could relive, it would be that one. The Last One. The one that has left her with such sorrow and guilt. She wouldn't be distracted by her work or getting to her office, she would feel every moment. She would memorize the colors and the way her coffee stung her throat when she swallowed. She would tattoo the look in Michael's eyes, the one that was only ever meant for her, to her heart. Yes, if she could relive any moment on Earth, it would be The Last One.

The Last Sunrise.

Chapter 14

"Who is that?" Liv nearly whispered to herself. Pulling her headphones off of her head, she set them gently on the table beside her. The noise of the house rushed toward her, the silence she had been immersed in since— *"Oh my goodness! It's six o'clock?"* Liv looked down at her notebook, where seventeen pages of handwritten words shone back up at her.

The Last Sunrise.

The work she'd done—the most she'd done since … well, since Michael died—distracted her for a moment from the figure she could see knocking on her side door. Shaking her head in amazement at all those words strung together, with a touch of confusion, she hurried to answer the knock.

"Hello?" she asked as she opened the door.

"Liv?" Josh said as he turned around, holding her coveted picnic basket. "I knocked a few times. Since you didn't answer, I was just going to leave this for you." His blue eyes shone with a touch of evening light, the wind rustled his blonde hair—and sent a flutter of excitement through Liv's heart.

"My picnic basket! I completely forgot! Oh my gosh, thank you so much. I'm sorry I didn't hear you." She gestured back toward her headphones on the table.

"No problem at all. I took the liberty of throwing out the leftovers—I didn't think you wanted old grapes and stale crackers?" He smiled. A smile that reached his eyes.

Liv laughed. "No, I guess I don't." She opened the door as wide as she could with one hand and reached for the basket with the other. Not committing to stepping outside and not inviting him in either. She left herself hanging in a limbo of her own making. And she wasn't sure why.

"Careful, it's kind of heavy," Josh said as he used both hands to hold the basket.

Tipping her head in question as to why an empty picnic basket would be heavy, Liv peeked in the top.

"My mom always taught me never to return a dish empty. I figured a picnic basket followed the same rules."

Liv laughed as she saw two small bottles of Pellegrino, a small container of sliced cheese, a sleeve of oat crackers, a bowl of strawberries, several drumsticks of fried chicken, and what looked like two oatmeal and dried cherry cookies from The Local Cup. A picnic. For two. Suddenly Liv's cheeks were mimosa pink. Again.

"My goodness, thank you." Her voice was quiet in response.

"I hope I'm not overstepping. I just thought maybe we could have lunch?" His smile was shy, unassuming.

Liv's belly fluttered to flight with a host of butterflies. Looking at her watch, Liv laughed. "Tomorrow?" she asked.

"Well, I had grand plans this morning of making it here by lunch. But, my mom had some doctor's appointments that went longer than I anticipated …"

"Is everything okay?"

"For today. The doctor is putting her through an entire battery of tests. Unfortunately, the longer I have been here—the more I see the confusion is, well … it's happening more often than I thought. I have a lot of decisions to make about her … the house."

"I'm sorry to hear that, Josh. I really am. Your mom was always so kind to me—and sassy! I always admired that about her!"

"She was. She still is, some of the time. Which, in part, is what makes this so hard. Confusion changes people." Josh's smile was one of resignation.

Suddenly, Liv realized that this man was standing

on her porch, awkwardly holding out a picnic basket full of food—her picnic basket!—and she had yet to ask him in. Her manners fought with thirty years of marriage as she debated what to do.

"You certainly don't have to eat with me, Liv. I didn't pack any alcohol on purpose—I thought about adding a bottle of wine, but I didn't want to add any pressure and I figured if you said no to me, at least you and Bella would have a meal."

"No, no, I'm actually hungry—I've actually … I've actually been working and haven't had a thing to eat in …" Liv checked her watch and realized she hadn't eaten since brunch with the ladies. "Well, in hours at least. It sounds good! Give me a minute, I'll be right out. I know the perfect spot."

And so Josh and Liv walked toward the bluff and the set of stairs that lead down to the beach.

"These stairs were built somewhere around 1930, and the house was built in 1928. I love the stone pillars—cement with native rocks on each one." Liv gave Josh a running commentary on her property as they walked, pointing out the mayapples and the ferns that covered the bluff, skirting the towering and spindly birch trees and majestic cedars. "The mayapples came from the woods around the house I grew up in, the ferns came from Michael's childhood home."

"Michael? Your husband?"

"Yes. Michael."

"Michael, who was in London?"

"Yes. Michael who was in London." Liv's heart began to race. She wasn't sure why she'd agreed to this picnic—other than that the pure spontaneity of it took her off guard enough she couldn't say no. That and those blue eyes which were so familiar and yet completely foreign at the same time. It wasn't as if she felt unsafe—after all she *did* know Josh. It was more that she felt … disloyal. Disloyal to Michael, and disloyal to her grief. Women in mourning don't have picnics on the bluff with men who … who look like Josh. Still, Liv couldn't deny it was nice to not feel lonely. And Josh was good company. Good *looking* company, too.

Walking down the steps with Josh made her feel how she had felt most of *that* summer. She knew it was dangerous, she knew it was a risk, she knew it was short lived but she also found she couldn't say no. She didn't *want* to say no. So she continued, putting one foot in front of the other.

The rest of the descent down to the water was quiet. Liv was acutely aware of the fact that Josh was steps behind her. She wondered if he was watching her. Did he think time had been kind to her? Did he wonder what happened to the girl she had been? Or could he see pieces of her in the woman in front of him? Liv's face flushed at her own thoughts as she cursed her skin.

The steps were many, but they finally made it to the landing where two red Adirondack chairs sat facing the blue water. The landing was nearly to the bottom of the stairs, which ended at the beach. The spot was perfect for a picnic.

"Here," she said, wiping the seat of both chairs free of pine needles and leaves with her hand. Josh busied himself opening the picnic and laying out the food and utensils. He was a slow worker, deliberate and precise—in direct contrast to Michael's quick and frantic pace. She noticed he wasn't wearing a wedding ring—she'd assumed he was single, and Lucy had insisted as much as well. But the mere absence of a small ring on his hand gave her butterflies—again.

"I wasn't joking when I said I had wondered what happened to you, Liv." Josh smiled.

Liv nodded. "It was a long time ago, wasn't it?"

Josh bobbed his head in agreement, popping a strawberry in his mouth. "How's Bella?"

"Bella is ... Bella." Liv took a slice of cheese and a cracker and added it to her plate. "She's not talking to me much these days."

"She'll come around."

"So, you told me about your kids. What about your

… wife?" A strange clench of wonder squeezed Liv's belly.

"No, no wife." He laughed. "Divorced. A long time ago."

"Ahh … it happens," Liv answered.

"Yes, it does. We met in college, got married, bought a house, had kids. We always just did the next thing and the next thing. I was happy enough. But apparently, she wasn't. And you know what? She was right. I would say we were way too young—and really weren't a good fit to begin with. We should never have gotten married. But then I wouldn't have Lacy and Zane"

"Your kids?"

"Yep. Hoping to get them to come up here before I leave but, you know, they are busy." Josh's eyes drifted out to the water. This time of the year the sky would be bright until nearly ten o'clock, but there was no denying the fading light of the day in the hazy lavender mist of the sky.

"Being a parent isn't for the faint of heart, is it?" Liv smiled.

"No it's not." Josh nodded his agreement. "Life is not for the faint of heart."

Liv nodded quietly. The sadness in his eyes as they looked out over the rolling water felt like a reflection of her own. Life was full of many heartaches, so many losses. One thing being a widow had done was hone her ability to see heartache. It was almost a superpower; she could see through the facade of happy people. She could see when people hurt even when they couldn't. It was as if her own heartache was so big it only recognized pain. Josh had lost his marriage, his brother, and his father, and was now losing his mother in the hardest of ways. It was no wonder sadness settled on him.

The pair sat quietly and watched the crystal blue water of the day fade to the inky pool of the night. They finished their chicken and strawberries and shared a cookie. They talked about the weather and his mother and her parents—her mother had moved to Arizona full time a year before Michael died and her father lived in Franklin. She hadn't stayed particularly close to either of them—and they hadn't bothered to stay close to her. It was as if Liv reminded them each of each other and neither of them were comfortable with that.

Liv would have expected to feel uncomfortable, sitting on the landing and talking with Josh. But instead, there was a quiet solace in sitting with a man who knew her when she was a young woman. A young woman with stars in her eyes and dreams and a whole life of opportunity in front of her. He didn't know her now. But he knew her then, and tonight that felt like all she needed.

"So, no wife. What about Angela? If you didn't hire her to sell your house …?" Once the words were out, she'd realized they sounded … curious. Like perhaps she was interested. And she wasn't interested. Not really. Maybe in a fantasy world, a world of what-if in her mind. *Was she?*

Josh laughed. "Angela. Let's see. Angela used to date my brother. I ran into her in town a few hours before the Kickoff and she asked if I wanted to go. So I went."

They both laughed a little bit, at Angela's expense. At the moment, when Angela was doused in lemonade, it felt funny. Now, under the evening sky, it felt juvenile.

"Poor Angela." Josh shook his head from side-to-side.

"Have you made any decisions about selling your mom's house?"

"I still haven't decided about the house, but I did agree to meet with Angela to have her look at the property."

Smiling, Liv shrugged her shoulders in laughter, tucking her hair behind her ears. She considered making a pitch for Lucy, but decided against it. "I'm hearing you haven't decided if you will sell your mom's house, but have you decided on … Angela?" *Where did that come from? Was she flirting with him? What was she doing?*

Josh let out a belly laugh that echoed down toward the water. "No decision to be made. She's a nice woman and I'm sure she's a fierce real estate agent. But she's not my type."

"You may want to tell her that," Liv shot back under her breath.

"I got that impression, yes." Josh shook his head and closed his eyes while he tipped his head back farther to laugh. Liv felt a jolt of pleasure at making him laugh.

"You were working when I got here. What do you do?" Josh asked.

Now, it was Liv's turn to laugh. Except, wait. She actually had gotten work done today. Well, she'd gotten words down on paper today. It very well may be that when she reads through them in the morning, she will decide they are awful, terrible, boring drivel and throw them away. But it was the most she had written in a very long time, and for that she was grateful.

A small pit of worry swirled in her belly at the thought of work and her unanswered call back to Isla. She would have to call her agent first thing in the morning. No questions asked. It was time to face the music.

"I am a writer. Romance novels. I am supposed to

be working on my first book of a new series. My deadline is in early September, and I am … let's say, I'm behind."

"I'm sure you'll catch up. Finish on time," he said with more confidence than he should have in her ability. For a moment his belief in her buoyed her spirits. Until she reminded herself that Josh had no idea. Outside of Frannie knowing she *may* sell the house so she can cure her writer's block, no one had any idea of the truth.

What if she told him? What if she told Josh, this familiar stranger? What if she told him the whole truth? Suddenly it made perfect sense. Because the truth of the matter is that he was already the holder of her deepest, darkest secret, and he had been for nearly thirty years.

Chapter 15

Bella slammed the steel mailbox door shut and turned to walk back toward the house. Either her mom had already grabbed the mail—which could be bad—or it hadn't been delivered yet, which would be good. Bella supposed she could ask her mom, but she had no intention of drawing attention to her interest in the mail by asking if it had arrived yet. That would only lead to questions—questions Bella did not want to answer. During these first few weeks at home, she had successfully avoided Liv and most of her questions. The Tequila Night could have been disastrous—but somehow, outside of the typical lecture on underage drinking (which Bella realized she deserved), it had actually served as a buffer.

It wasn't that Liv was ignoring Bella. No, quite the opposite. She was ever-present, just not intrusive. Her trademark method of peppering her daughter with questions as if her daily activities were worthy of a

Spanish Inquisition was gone. Liv simply existed, pleasantly, next to Bella. It was weird. And although Bella claimed to want her mom to back off, the lack of questioning left Bella feeling oddly neglected.

Bella was only a few yards from the mailbox when Liv turned the corner onto the gravel driveway, returning from her run, and headed right for her daughter. Olivia swiftly turned off her watch timer and plucked her headphones out of her ears. "Good morning, sweet pea!" she yelled while waving a hand above her head. "It's beautiful out here! I got an early start—the sunrise was fantastic!"

Her mother approached her with all the enthusiasm finishing an early morning run will give you, and Bella winced as Liv's arms circled her shoulders. Bella ached to hug her father. Her bones literally felt weaker, her muscles knotted and her belly sick at the wanting. You would think that a hug from her mother would be the next best answer. It wasn't, and Bella couldn't explain why. She found a twisted satisfaction in rebuffing her mom's nurturing advances. And while it felt good in the moment, she knew the minute her mom walked away, the shame and embarrassment at what a brat she was would surface. Still, she twisted out of Liv's grasp and walked toward the house alone, staying a few steps ahead of her mom—who was still cooling down.

Summer Love

"I was just grabbing something from my car," Bella lied.

Liv tilted her head as parents do.

Bella had nothing in her arms and was coming from the opposite side of the house from where her Jeep was parked. Seeing her misstep a fraction of a second too late, Bella began to backtrack. "It wasn't there. I was looking for my sunglasses. I wanted to make sure I hadn't lost them. But they weren't there. I'll have to go look in my room." Bella knew she was rambling. She knew she'd just given herself away. By not keeping her lie simple and adding too much detail, she'd just set off Liv's mom radar. Still, she walked quickly into the house and straight into the bathroom before Liv could question her.

"Hey, Bella! I'm going to make myself an omelet for breakfast. You hungry?"

Yes. Yes, she was starving. But an omelet meant sitting at the island next to her mom for breakfast, and she simply couldn't handle a million questions this morning. "No, I already ate," she bellowed back from inside the bathroom, adding a tepid, "Thanks, though," when the guilt started to come.

Upstairs, Bella readied herself for work. She actually had the morning off, but she couldn't stay in this house for one more minute. She pulled on her blue Beyond

Blooms T-shirt and wrestled her hair up into a high ponytail. She swiped a little lotion on her face and added a touch of blush and some mascara, tucked a tube of ChapStick in her pocket, and was ready to go. She pulled her bedroom door shut tight, making a clear signal to Liv to stay out, and walked down the hallway.

At first she thought the ringing phone was her own—but when she pulled it out of her back pocket, it wasn't. Instead, she realized it was her mom's, ringing from her nightstand. Taking a deep breath and realizing she'd been a massive pain in the tail, she walked into her mom's room—something she hadn't done very often since her dad died—and quickly retrieved the phone in an effort to do something nice for her mom.

She caught sight of the walk-in closet as she turned, the familiar sight of her father's favorite jeans hanging on a hook (he never folded a thing!) and his work flannels organized by color (by Olivia—Michael was not nearly that organized) was replaced with an empty wall. His clothes were gone. She tiptoed into the closet a few steps further, feeling both a right to be there and also as if she was an intruder.

Gone. His clothes were gone.

She knew in her mind that of course, his clothes couldn't stay there forever. She knew her mom likely donated them to a charity for people in need—Bella remembered a snippet of a conversation where Liv had mentioned something about that. She also knew that her heart was consumed with hurt and betrayal at the erasure of her father from this house. First, Liv had some strange man here the night she got drunk, and now every stitch of clothing from her father had disappeared. Bella did not like the way this was going.

Liv's phone had long since stopped ringing in Bella's hand, and now a voicemail chimed through. Bella's heart nearly stopped when she saw the name: Coach Cooper.

Bella's hands immediately got sweaty, her breath pulling in and out quickly from her chest. Coach Cooper. From U of M. Quickly and without thinking, she opened her mom's phone (she hadn't changed her passcode since Bella was young—it was and still is her dad's birthday) and opened the voicemail app. She could hear Liv downstairs, singing along to the Kings of Leon—her dad's favorite band—as she cooked in the kitchen. Grateful for her mother's distraction, Bella lifted the phone to her ear to hear what Coach Cooper had to say.

"Hey there, Mrs. Pennington. This is Coach Cooper from U of M. I was just calling this morning regarding Bella. I need to touch base with you—I have a few things I'm concerned about. Please give me a call at—"

Bella turned off the phone and deleted the message, and quickly deleted the missed call. That was the very last thing she needed: her mother talking to Coach Coop. Taking the stairs two at a time, Bella jumped off the last two and breezed into the kitchen with a smile on her face.

"Hey, Mom, I saw your phone. Grabbed it for ya." She smiled.

"Oh … thanks, honey! I thought I heard it ringing. I guess I didn't realize I left it upstairs." Liv continued to plate her veggie omelet and smiled up at her daughter.

"No, it wasn't ringing. That was mine."

"Headed to work already? I thought you didn't have to work until noon today?"

"Yes, well no. First I am having breakfast with Hannah—that's who called—then work at noon." Bella looked at her phone clock quickly. "Actually, I'm running late. I better go."

Just as Bella opened the door, Frannie was stepping in. "Mornin' y'all! Where you headed so fast, Miss Bella? Seems like I only ever see you comin' and goin'!"

"Breakfast with Hannah!" Bella quickly hugged Frannie and waved to her mom. "See you guys! Have good days!" And she was off.

"Morning, Fran." Liv smiled, tucking her hair behind her ear as she sat down to eat her breakfast. She offered to make another omelet, but Frannie declined. The two friends talked about what was on the docket for the day—Frannie was replacing the faucet in the kitchen sink (*thank goodness! The drip-drip-drip was relentless!*) and had picked up a few new cupboard tracks to repair the two drawers in the half bathroom that weren't sliding correctly. She'd also get started painting the guest bedroom. A soft shade of gray.

Liv half-heartedly listened as Frannie explained an issue with a part for the washing machine, which had also gone on the fritz. "Hey, girl, are you listenin' to me?" Frannie finally asked, her Irish green eyes playing perfectly off of her milky white skin and auburn hair.

"I'm sorry. I'm anxious this morning. I was up most of the night and finally got out of bed and went for a run at five. Eight miles later I finally made myself run home. I have to call Isla today. I can't avoid it any longer."

"Isla? Isla your agent?"

Liv nodded her head yes. "She thinks I have a book ready. Well, almost ready." Liv let out a scoff. "Actually, that's probably not even true. By my ignoring her phone calls, texts, and emails, I am sure she has realized that I do not, in fact, have a book ready."

"Writer's block," Frannie said, finally putting all the pieces together. Well, almost all.

"I'm scared."

"Do you want me to sit here while you call?" Frannie asked, stepping toward her life-long friend, her perfectly manicured brows seamed together in worry.

"No, no I think it's something I need to do myself. I haven't been honest with her, and it's time I fess up to my writer's block and the fact that I have virtually zero words written for this new book." Under Liv's hand sat the notebook, the cover closed, that held the seventeen hand-written pages she'd worked through yesterday.

She'd been up reading and re-reading them most of the night, and had even added some to it. But the problem was, this writing, these words—they weren't fiction. They were her life. They were the love story of Michael and Liv. They were not for public consumption. And so while she was thrilled to be writing—anything—again, she was still no closer to solving her problem. She had no plot, no characters, and no hope.

"She'll understand, won't she? Y'all are close. Always have been."

Liv looked to the ceiling. Those words stung. They were close. When Isla had first taken Liv on as a client, the two did become fast friends, and they were a formidable pair in the industry. Isla had deserved so much more than she'd given her.

"It's not just about Isla. It's …" Liv paused. Her eyes threatened to fill with tears and her throat closed tightly. She just couldn't bear to tell Frannie about the money. She had to figure something out. Michael had worked his entire adult life to be sure they were financially secure. Sure, Liv had contributed significantly to her current financial situation. But Michael was the one who was gone. And any financial difficulty that came to Liv and Bella would be placed on Michael's behalf. Liv couldn't abide by it.

Frannie rubbed Liv's back as she spoke. "Sounds like you have been keeping a few secrets. Maybe it's time to tell everybody the truth?"

"The thing is, Frannie. When I make this phone call, I won't have a choice. The truth will be all I have. And the truth won't be enough to save my career, or this house, or … my relationship with my daughter."

Chapter 16

Josh reached for a towel off the top rack of the laundry room closet. He listened closely for any footsteps upstairs. His mom had yet to get up this morning, and while he didn't want her to worry if he was gone when she did wake up, he didn't want to wake her unnecessarily either. So he went old school. Pulling a pencil and paper out of the junk drawer in the corner of the kitchen, he jotted Dorothy a quick note and headed out toward the water.

Ruby, his mom's King Charles Cavalier, came prancing into the room, staring up at him with her big doe eyes.

"Ahh. You're hungry, aren't you, little girl?" He pulled out a can of dog food from the fridge, dumping the second half of it into Ruby's bowl for breakfast.

"There ya go, girl. Enjoy." Josh quietly closed the door behind him as he left the house for the beach.

The sun was bright—and hot—already this morning. With no breeze in the air, a swim was the perfect substitute for his typical run. He threw the towel up toward the house and waded in, letting the cold water wash over his feet and help to wake him up.

He'd been restless last night, unable to sleep. Dorothy had become confused enough on the way home from the doctor's office that he'd had a heart-stopping moment where he wasn't sure she knew who he was. She'd recovered, but the fear in her eyes and the worry in his was enough that he decided to follow up with the doctor this morning concerning the tests they had run. He had a feeling he was going to have to reach some decisions earlier rather than later and he had no idea where to start.

Damnit, Justin. I wish you were here, he thought. It was not supposed to be this way. He wasn't supposed to be the only one left.

He made his way out into the water far enough to be able to dive in and took the plunge. The cold and silence washed over him as he counted strokes and breaths, consulting his watch occasionally for time and distance. When he'd reached the halfway point, he stood up and stretched, arching his back and lifting his face up toward the sun.

It wasn't just his mom that was on his mind. Dinner with Olivia had sparked something in him. A desire. He wanted to see her again, but wasn't sure what the rules were. Still, she'd shared a meal with him by the beach. That had to mean something?

He shook his head to dislodge water in his ears as he dove back in. His mind returned to counting, kicks, strokes, and breaths in rhythmic patterns. Yep, swimming had been the perfect antidote to his troubles this morning.

When he'd finished his distance, he floated on his back, letting the warm sun and cold water mix together like blue and red watercolor paint. His heart wanted to see Liv. There was no denying that. In between worrying about his mom through the night, long ago memories of the summer he'd spent with Liv had resurfaced. He wondered if she'd want to go *out* to dinner sometime. She'd seemed both timid and self-assured in his presence, so he wasn't sure which way an invitation would go.

There was only one way to figure it out.

Standing in the kitchen with the towel wrapped around his waist, Josh listened again. This time he could hear the soft pitter-patter of his mom getting ready for the day upstairs, so he quietly grabbed his cell phone and stepped back onto the back porch.

"Is Dr. Cameron in, please?" he asked. "This is Joshua Hart, calling about my mom, Dorothy Hart's, test results."

Josh waited as the receptionist connected him to the right line. Fully anticipating leaving a voicemail, he was surprised when Dr. Cameron herself answered.

"Hi there, Josh. How are you?"

"I'm well. Thank you. The reason for my call this morning was that my mom had another ... spell? Episode? I don't know what to call it. But she was confused on our way home yesterday, and then, when she looked at me ... well, I am not sure that she knew who I was. I was just curious if you had any of the results back yet?"

"Actually, yes. You were on my list to call today, which is why my receptionist put you straight through. I think I have some answers for us, but they aren't as positive as we'd like to see."

"Oh?" Josh's hands began to shake, just a touch.

"Your mom has what we call vascular dementia. It's typically, a result of damage from strokes—"

"But she hasn't had any strokes?"

"Well, actually, I can see some evidence of a few small strokes your mom has suffered. She's been living alone for a while, correct?"

"How could she have had a stroke and I not know it?"

"Well, I know it seems hard to believe. But it can happen."

Dr. Cameron spent the next twenty minutes explaining Dorothy's medical condition, prognosis, and treatments. None of which was good news.

"All in all, she's going to need full-time care when you leave. I have plenty of resources here in my office to help you make that decision. In fact, I have a colleague, Tara Sanders, whose only job *is* to help facilitate those changes for families. I will have her give you a call to schedule a time to consult and help you decide on next steps."

"And in the meantime?" Josh asked, his voice sounding even smaller than he felt.

"In the meantime, keep her safe by eliminating fall risks—things like loose throw rugs or items left on the floor. Part of what Tara will do is to evaluate home safety and she can help you keep the house safe for as long as you will be here. Do you know how long that will be?"

"I'm staying for the summer." Suddenly, all the worry and uncertainty of the morning came down to one resounding and frankly easy decision. All the things he was thinking about this morning—his mom, the house, Liv—the only way to find answers was to stay here for the summer. He had until September to figure it all out.

Chapter 17

"And?" Frannie asked as Liv walked back into the kitchen. Liv had seen Frannie nervously watching as she paced back and forth on the edge of the bluff, tracing the property line of the house as she spoke to Isla on the phone. It had been forty-seven minutes since Liv had walked outside to call Isla, and for all forty-seven minutes Frannie had gotten exactly nothing done.

"I knew this was coming." Liv's eyes held no tears, no emotion at all really. "It's not a surprise. I mean, they gave me the advance to write a book. And I haven't written a book …"

"What do you mean? You are talking book-speak, and I'm from Georgia. I don't understand it."

"The publisher is terminating my contract and I have to return my advance if I don't come up with a book by September first. I have to sell the house."

"But you have written dozens of best sellers for them!" Frannie answered. "That hardly seems fair that your husband dies and they can't give you time?"

"They have given me time, Fran. They have given me two years. It's my own fault. I should have budgeted better, I should have buckled down, I should have written …" Her voice faded off as her hand reached out for the notebook on the counter. Fanning the pages from front to back, Liv could see the hours of work she'd produced yesterday. She had been filled with so much hope—for the first time in a long time she thought maybe she'd recaptured the magic she'd always had when it came to writing. But this morning she'd realized that she had been wrong.

The words, they were beautiful. And moving and true. And that was the problem. She was a novelist, a romance writer. No one would be interested in a memoir of the love—and loss—of her life. She was out of time.

"There has to be something we can do. Together. You, me, Lucy, and Maggie. We just need to sit at the round table together, and you need to tell them the truth. They can't find you if you don't tell them where you are at," Frannie said.

"I'm right here! I am right here in my kitchen! My kitchen with a leaky sink and the doorknob that fell off! My kitchen that Michael and I designed together. The kitchen I'm going to lose. I'm not hard to find, Frannie. I'm right here. In the same place I have been since the day Michael died. Right. Here." Liv covered her eyes with her hands, frustration coming in fast.

"Liv, I love you. You know that. That's not what I'm talking about, and you know it. They—Lucy and Maggie—can't help you if they can't find you and they can't find you if you don't tell them the truth."

"The truth." Liv laughed. "The truth is, I have spent two years ignoring my job, spending money that was advanced to me and … I have to give it back." Liv groaned as she sat down on the stool and put her head in her hands.

"I don't understand, Liv. I thought Michael had an insurance policy?"

"He did. But when Michael died, we had a lot of debt." Liv refused to pick her head up out of her hands. "We had taken a loan out on the house so he could float the development project he had just taken on—Hawk's Ridge north of Franklin? Yeah. I sold the land after he died, but I lost money and was left with a pretty large loan on the house. I haven't worked in two years, Bella's scholarship covers very little of her expenses. I have money left—but I need money to live now that my writing career is in the tank."

"Even more reason why we need to tell Lucy and

Maggie. We need help. We can solve this, but it's going to take all of us."

Liv sat quietly for a few minutes.

"Oh my gosh, how am I going to tell Bella? She's going to be furious." Liv whimpered as she rocked her head back and forth.

"She's a kid. She'll be mad; she's spicy like that. But darlin', she's starting out on her own life. She doesn't even live here full time anymore! She will be okay—"

"I don't know, Frannie. I don't. She's already ... I don't know. There's something up. I mean, first Josh and I caught her passed out drunk, and she mostly ignores any suggestion I have for us to spend time together. This morning she was out checking the mailbox when I came home from my run."

"So, she's checkin' the mail?" Frannie asked, eyebrows raised.

"Well, I watched her check the mail—which was silly. It was way too early to be delivered yet. And then when I asked what she was doing, she said she was getting something from her car—which was on the other side of the house. She lied. For no reason."

"She's been on her own for a long time, Liv. Nine months! Give her a minute, she's had a lot of changes lately."

"I don't know. That's what Josh said, too. But I'm

telling you that something isn't right ... it's just my mother's intuition, but I am pretty sure I'm right." Liv was adamant. Frannie looked closely at Liv, and Liv's stomach clenched. Had she just mentioned Josh for a *second* time in one conversation?

"Well, I'm not a mom," Frannie said as she walked toward the fridge to grab some water. "So, I can't go speakin' to that. But I can tell you that we—your friends—are here to help you. But you gotta tell everybody the truth." Frannie's words were softened by her southern accent, but her intent was clear. She'd had enough.

The thought of telling her friends—her best friends—how badly she had mismanaged her life, her career, her finances and her daughter felt not just hard, but impossible. As if the words that refused to make it to the page would also betray her if she tried to tell them what was really going on. There had to be another answer.

"I hear you, I do. But can you just give me a few more weeks, Frannie? Because the truth is, I have to settle things with Bella first. She has to be the first one to know about the house. You are the only one who knows ... knows it all. Please, I'm just asking for a few more weeks to make it right with Bella. In fact—I gotta run." With that, Liv reached up and kissed Frannie on the cheek and hugged her. "I love you, Fran."

"I love you too, Liv. I'll give you a week. Just one. Then I'm done keepin' the peace."

Chapter 18

The sounds of a lawn mower engine filled Liv's car as she pulled into the driveway and parked. She wasn't exactly sure why she had ended up here. In fact, she wasn't entirely sure how she remembered where to go. The house was one of the larger cottages—large enough not to qualify as a cottage, actually—just north of town. Liv had always admired it the few times she'd been on the water. It stood tall on the soft, rounded edge of a hill—quite different from her own bluff, but was nearly hidden from the road. It was white with dark emerald-green shutters and trim, and the porch wrapped from the roadside clear around to the front, giving an expansive view of the lake. She took a deep breath, smelling the distinctly summer scent of cut grass with its sweet tang.

The house had fallen into some level of disrepair.

"I know the feeling, old girl," she said to the house as she looked up toward the widow's watch at the top. Suddenly a small black dog came skirting around from the lake side yard, barking ferociously. Of course, given her size she wasn't all that scary, but still Liv took a step back out of respect. Within seconds the sounds of the mower stopped, and all of a sudden Josh was standing just a few feet away.

"Hey, Liv …" He wore a white T-shirt, blue jeans, and a baseball cap backward. A sheen of sweat covered his arms as he stood with one hand on his hip. Liv caught her breath. Today, in the early afternoon sunlight, it was like looking into a kaleidoscope; she could see both the young boy she'd known and the man who stood before her. Right down to the way he stood. The grin on his face and the butterflies that had taken flight in her stomach.

"I'm sorry to bother you—" Liv broke her sentence off, choosing not to compete with the pup who still felt she was a threat and had yet to stop barking.

"Ruby! Ruby, she's okay. Come on, go inside." Josh bent easily to scoop up the little dog. He ran up the porch stairs and deposited her inside the front door. "Sorry about that, she's my mom's pride and joy. And she's also not used to company."

"She's cute." Liv smiled. "I like her chutzpah."

Josh let out a belly laugh, tipping his head up toward the sun. Liv's smile was spontaneous. It felt good to make him laugh again. She remembered the feeling from their picnic dinner, it dawned on her that it must be important, making someone laugh. She hadn't done that much since Michael died. The feeling felt familiar, and gave rise to a giddy laughter inside her own chest.

"That she does have! Not a whole lot of sense, but chutzpah in spades." Josh quietly returned his gaze toward Liv, waiting.

"I was wondering if we could talk? If you have time?" Liv asked.

The path down to the water was the exact opposite of Liv's. He lived farther up the coastline, where the bluff settled into a gentle rolling hill instead of the shearing cliff it is south of town. On top of that, the beach on this end of town was deeper, with less rock and more sand this summer than hers. One of the curious things about living on the coast was how the landscape was ever changing. Next summer, she could be the benefactor of a deeper beach. Or at least, the new owner's would be.

"How's your mom today?" Liv asked, stalling.

"She's tired. Napping at the moment."

Liv looked in Josh's direction, the sun shining just perfectly to show his eyes pulled together.

"Is something wrong?"

Josh took a deep sigh. "I spoke with the doctor this morning. They found evidence of past strokes, which have led to vascular dementia. Essentially, Alzheimer's that progresses more quickly."

"Oh Josh, I'm so sorry to hear that."

"I knew it was something. And I know I should be grateful. She's lived a long life. It's just ... hard."

"I can imagine it is." Liv reached up to squeeze his arm. The warmth she found was welcome, and she didn't want to let go.

"She's kind of let the house go these past few years, so I'm trying to take on a few projects while I'm here—at the house and on the boat. Get a few things done. It's different than the work I do in my office. It's like … instant gratification. The grass is long—I mow it—it looks better." Josh smiled.

"Instant gratification is powerful," Liv answered. "You have a lot on your plate—"

"Everyone has a lot on their plate," he answered. "What did you need to talk about, Liv? I'm all ears."

While the decision to see Josh and ask for his advice had come without thought, now, in his presence she felt much like the young girl the summer the two met. He'd been older, and he had felt wiser. She'd felt protected in a time when she felt the most vulnerable—when her family fell apart.

Maybe that's why she came back to him now. She thought again about the relief she felt when he helped her with Bella on the porch. She was tired of the echo chamber in her own mind. Yes, she wanted relief. But she also wanted help. Their footsteps fell into a rhythm, his long-paced step slowing to her shorter, quicker ones. She remembered this about him. He was patient. That summer they had walked miles upon miles together, Josh listening and Liv talking. She'd never felt pressured or pushed. He created a space of welcome quiet—a refuge from what was a chaotic and difficult season of her life.

"I have to sell my house," Liv said. She had decided to start there and work her way around the problem she had created.

Josh turned and looked at her. Where her eyes had stayed mostly dry with Frannie, now, they pooled with tears. He took his hand and reached for hers, lacing their fingers together easily. The warmth from his hand felt good, like her hand on his arm, but it was the weight of it inside her own that felt safe. Their arms touched as they walked, sending jolts of—Liv didn't know what—through her body. The heat from the rising sun was coming, but the heat from Josh was different in a familiar, nostalgic way. Her heart raced.

"I have to sell my house because two years ago, right before Michael died, I accepted an advance for this new series I am supposed to be writing. I don't know what you know about the publishing world—but the advance isn't really an advance. It's a ... loan. The money for the advance comes from book sales. And ... I don't have a book to sell," her voice was quiet.

Josh squeezed her hand, holding on tighter now. Waves lapped up onto the sand, washing away their footprints as quickly as they appeared. The water, still cold from a winter full of ice, would take until August before the townsfolk would declare it warm. Although, the temperature wouldn't keep many of them from jumping in.

"I already spent the advance. My deadline is the first week in September, and there is no way, no conceivable way for me to produce a book by then." Her tears were falling freely now. "I don't know what to do. Bella will be so angry with me—she already is angry with me, and I don't even know why. Now I'm going to give her another reason to hate me."

"Hey, hey, hey, come here." Josh stopped and pulled Liv toward him. He wrapped his arms around the top of her shoulders, and she fit neatly into the space under his chin. Her head rested on his chest, rising and falling with each breath he took. In a moment, she was sixteen again, finding comfort in the boy from the dock. The boy who wasn't Michael.

"I don't know how this all happened. I really don't.

I only know that I've lost my husband and my career—now I'm going to lose my house *and* my daughter."

Josh let her cry. Her nose was runny, and her eyes were pink. And then, he unwrapped his arms, grabbed her hand, and started walking.

"Forward motion is always better than standing still—even if it's messy," Josh said.

Liv nodded. She understood that perhaps better than anyone. "I ran eight miles at five a.m. this morning." She laughed.

"I was up at five, too," he added. "You aren't going to lose Bella."

"I don't know. She's pretty short with me now, who knows what she will do when she finds out I've lost the house."

"Liv, it sounds to me that *you* didn't lose the house. It's just life. Things change. I don't mean to sound flippant, certainly not about you losing your husband. But life changes. Our circumstances change. In fact, the reality is that life is really just a long line of challenges strung together with ordinary days in between. Bella will understand. Maybe not at first, but she will."

"I don't know what to do," Liv said.

Josh nodded his head. "I understand that completely."

He squeezed her hand and walked a few more steps

before he pulled them both out into the surf. They walked into the gentle oncoming waves until they were in up to their knees. The water was freezing, but also felt alive. Each step breathed life back into Liv. They continued to hold hands, taking big deep breaths of the seascape.

"When I'm in Detroit, I forget how breathtaking this view is. I mean, we have the river downtown—but it's not this," Josh said with a chuckle.

"Do you know how many people who visit here are surprised you can't see across the lake?" Liv asked.

Josh laughed. "I know, it's funny, isn't it? Is it because it's named *Lake* Huron? I love the ocean, but there is something about the big lakes. The fresh water, it's healing."

Liv took a deep pull of summer air. *Healing.* As hard as this all was, as awful as it felt to lose her house and her book contract, she could not deny a nagging feeling of hope. As if the weight of the impending doom was heavier than the actual disaster. She had worried about the book, the contract, the lien, the house for so long she was surprised to find that in the middle of that ball of emotional yarn was a thread of relief.

Was she finally healing? She shook her head at the thought. She would *never* be over losing Michael. She could never let that happen. But still, the small bubble of hope that maybe she could learn to live with it began to float. Could she heal and *not* forget?

"What are you going to do about your mom?" Liv asked.

"I'm not sure yet."

"Sounds like we're in the same boat." Liv laughed.

Josh smiled and squeezed her hand. "I guess we are. Liv, I don't know if you are a spiritual person. In reality, I know very little of the woman you are now. I am so glad you felt you could come to me, but I don't know if I'm the right person to help you. Of course, I'll do whatever I can. Actually I have an idea."

Liv squinted her eyes in question.

"When my brother died, I lost my best friend and my business partner. He was always my go-to when I needed advice or help. I was so lost at first, like I couldn't make a decision. I would try and imagine what he would tell me to do, and frankly, most of the time I think I already knew. But what really helped was when I talked to him. I'd go for a run and just talk to him. What if you talked to Michael? What if you threw your faith in him out into the world and asked him to help you?" Josh quietly let go of her hand, nodding his chin out toward the vast horizon.

Josh walked back up to the waterline where their footsteps had been completely erased by the relentless waves and sat down in the dry line of sand to wait. Liv stared at the sand where their footsteps used to be. Is that what happens? You live and love and walk upon this Earth and then time simply erases who you were? No, Liv didn't believe that. She turned her face toward the rising sun, took a deep breath, and began.

"Michael, there's something I need to tell you …"

Chapter 19

"I hereby call this meetin' of the Ladies of the Round Table to order!" Frannie proclaimed as she sat down at the reserved round table near the front windows of The Local Cup.

"We can't start yet!" Maggie countered. "Lucy is running late, and I don't see a single mimosa at this table."

"Hannah? Can we get our usual?" Liv asked Hannah, who was just walking up. Liv's knee jumped up and down in anticipation. She had promised Frannie today would be the day. Today she would tell Maggie and Lucy she had to sell the house, and why. She hadn't had a chance to talk to Bella yet, but at the rate they were going, that chance might never come. Between Bella avoiding Liv, and Liv avoiding telling Bella the truth, the two were set on parallel courses that never crossed. After Josh had encouraged Liv to talk to Michael on the beach, she'd felt more settled. Josh had been right. She didn't need Michael to tell her what to do, she had just needed to tell Michael what was wrong. Still, admitting to her daughter and her friends what a mess she made would be hard, and she wasn't looking forward to it.

"Of course, Mrs. Pennington. There will be the four of you, right?" Hannah asked.

"Yes, honey. Thank you!" Liv answered. "There, now that that is settled, how are you, Maggie? I see Frannie all the time these days, I haven't seen you in a week!"

"I'm good. Boys are … good. Done with school for the summer, thank goodness. It will be a relief to not cringe every time I see the school's number on my phone for a few months."

"Oh bless yer heart. Those boys are somethin' else!" Frannie squeezed her friend's hand. "Bruce being helpful at all?"

"Ahhh … no. He's not. We are currently arguing about who's paying for day camp. He wants me to take them to the store with me instead of paying for camp—"

"Seriously? He did not say that. No way!" Liv answered.

"Oh yes, I'm serious. He wants no part of paying for childcare for them this summer. Says they are old enough to 'help out' at the store. Clearly, he doesn't spend enough time with them. And he hasn't been in my store. I'm so busy that Kevin and Bella and I can hardly keep up. Can you imagine me trying to watch my boys *and* run my business?"

Frannie started to cackle. "How is he possibly so out of touch?"

"I guess that's what happens when you have kids later in life and *then* decide to have a mid-life crisis that includes a mistress nearly half your age. It's whatever. Beyond Blooms is doing well, and I can afford it—"

"It doesn't matter if you can afford it or not!" Liv exclaimed. "They are *his* kids. He should help."

"Oh no, are we talking about Bruce the Jerk?" Lucy asked as she breezed into her seat. "What has he done now?"

"Same ol', same ol'. I don't even want to repeat it. Moving on!" Maggie smiled. "Hi, Luce, glad you could fit us in!"

"Oh stop, I will always fit my girls in. I am just ridiculously busy right now at work. Seems everyone wants a cottage on our Fresh Coast!"

"Sorry to interrupt, here are your mimosas, ladies!" Hannah placed a champagne glass down for each friend.

"Just what we need!" Lucy exclaimed.

"Thank you, Hannah!" Liv said. "By the way, did

you and Bella have fun at breakfast the other morning?"

"Me?" Hannah asked.

"Umm, yes, you? Didn't you guys have breakfast?"

"Umm … no, we didn't, Mrs. Pennington. Actually, I haven't seen Bella since she's been back. I texted her a few times to hang out, but she never … well we just haven't connected."

"Oh …" Liv looked at Frannie, her lips twisting in confusion. Hadn't Bella said she was having breakfast with Hannah the other day? And didn't she say she was with Hannah on Tequila Night? "I must have misunderstood! She must have said she was *going* to text you for breakfast."

Hannah nodded and smiled, asking if there was anything else the table needed before she walked away. As soon as she was out of sight, Liv dropped her head into her hands and shook it back and forth. "For the love of all things holy," Liv said. "I do not understand. At all."

"What do you mean? What's up?" Lucy asked.

"Miss Bella is making a habit out of not exactly tellin' the truth. Last week when I was at Liv's, Bella flew out of the house in a hurry—said she was meeting Hannah for breakfast before work," Frannie answered, her voice quiet, keeping the Ladies' business the Ladies' business.

"Frannie, one lie doesn't mean she's making a habit out of it—" Maggie started.

"It's not just the lie about breakfast. She's been behaving strangely. The other morning I was sure I heard my phone ring but when she brought it to me I had no missed calls or voicemails. She will say she's doing one thing, but it's obvious she's doing another …" Liv's voice faded. "Maggie, is she actually showing up to work?"

"Of course!" Maggie answered, quickly and with a touch too much volume.

Liv raised her eyebrows and tilted her head. "I would assume you would tell me the truth if she was giving you problems at work?"

"Well of course I would," Maggie answered, reaching for her mimosa. Her hand, visibly shaking, knocked over the glass, sending most of the champagne across the table. Hannah appeared nearly instantly with a rag to clean up the mess. "I'm so sorry, Hannah. I'm such a klutz!" All four women worked to lift glasses and move silverware so that Hannah had an easy time of cleaning. When she left, Liv turned to Maggie again.

"Maggie … do you know what's going on with Bella?"

Maggie continued to wipe at the table in front of her with a napkin. "I know that *something* is going on with Bella, yes."

"Do you know what that *something* is?" Liv asked more forcefully than she intended. Frannie and Lucy sat quietly. Since Michael died, Liv had been a pastel version of her vibrant self, and this spark of anger was more emotion than she had expressed in ages.

"Liv, I think you need to talk to Bella," Maggie answered.

"I have *tried* to talk to Bella. I have stayed out of Bella's way, I have given Bella space, and I have asked her to do things with me and given her free range to do everything she does without me. I have done everything I can think of to give her the time and space to come to *me*, and she hasn't. What do you know?" Each of the last four words was said with force and pause.

Maggie folded her hands in her lap and looked Liv in the eye. "She told me she dropped out of school."

"What?" Liv's voice was nearly a whisper. "She told you she did *what*?"

"Liv, she told me she dropped out of school." Maggie held her gentle eyes to Liv's fiery ones.

"And you didn't tell me this, why?" Liv asked.

"I told Bella she needed to tell you herself. I told her I would tell you if she didn't. I was trying to give her time."

"Meanwhile, I am floundering over here trying to

figure out what's wrong with *my* daughter! Maggie! How could you keep this from me?"

"I didn't mean to, Liv. I really didn't. I thought it was best to come from her, not me." Liv refused to look Maggie in the eye. And Maggie's deep blue eyes pooled with tears. "Liv, I'm so sorry. I know we don't keep secrets. I know. But … there's something else."

Liv tucked a lock of hair behind her ear and turned and looked at Maggie. Frannie and Lucy sat stock still.

"What?"

"What she told me was that she dropped out of school. But … I don't think that's true."

Liv looked at Maggie, both women's eyes full with tears. Lucy leaned in, looking to Liv like she would be ready to mediate at any moment, while Frannie sat back in her seat, trying to stay out of harm's way.

"Why don't you think that's true, Maggie?" Liv finally asked, her voice quiet and cold.

"Because I found this on the counter under my register this week." Maggie reached into her purse and pulled out a wrinkled paper and handed it to Liv.

Slowly, Liv opened the tightly creased paper. Her eyes scanned the words quickly. Her shoulders slumped forward as she realized what she was reading.

"You're right, Maggie. She didn't drop out. My daughter failed out of college."

Chapter 20

"Liv!" Lucy called. "Liv!" When Olivia didn't answer or slow down, Lucy finally demanded, "Olivia Pennington, stop."

Liv turned around quickly to face her friend. "What? What do you want?" After reading Bella's abysmal—and it was abysmal—report card Liv had thrown a twenty-dollar bill on the top of the round table and left The Local Cup without a word. Her intention was to go next door and confront Bella, but common sense—and fear—told her a public confrontation with Bella over a private matter would go as well as the Ladies of the Round Table meeting did this morning. Badly.

"I want you to stop walking so fast. I'm wearing heels for goodness' sakes," Lucy quipped.

"As if you couldn't run a marathon in those heels."

"Well, of course I could. But I don't want to today. I've got another showing this afternoon and I can't be

Summer Love

... sweaty," Lucy said with the perfect amount of arrogance and humility. "Besides, there is no reason to *run* today, Liv. None."

"So you don't think one of your best friends keeping a secret—a very large, life-changing secret—about your daughter is reason to be angry?" Liv shot back.

"I didn't say that." Lucy's voice was patient, and to Liv's frustrated ear sounded a little bit condescending. "I just said there is no reason to run. Or walk so fast."

"I'm so angry," Liv answered.

"I'm sure you are." Lucy motioned to a bench underneath a weeping willow tree centered in the town square. One of the things Liv loved about Blue Water Bay—and one thing Lucy made a good living selling—was the hometown feel of this small town, town center included. But today was different.

The two friends walked in silence until they reached the bench. Lucy sat first, pointing at the bench, giving Liv no excuse not to sit.

"I don't even know what happened to my life," Liv said, the fury of just a few moments ago gone as quickly as the sun behind a cloud. "I was going along just fine—wonderfully, actually. Michael was doing well, Bella was happy, and my books were selling. And then one morning I forget to pay attention, and it's all—" Liv took a big heaping pull of air to settle the oncoming sobs—"gone. It's all gone, Lucy, and there's nothing I can do about it."

"This sounds to me like you're talking about something more than just Bella failing out of school?" Lucy questioned.

Taking a deep breath and letting go of the sobs lodged in her throat, Olivia cried. She cried while the gentle summer breeze soothed her hard edges, and she cried until she felt like she could finally speak. And then, Olivia Pennington told her oldest friend in the world about the house, the lien, the advance, her contract—all of it. Lucy listened quietly, nodding in agreement or shaking her head with dismay.

"I wondered about the lien on the house after Michael died. I nearly asked you a dozen times. I brokered that deal with Michael, his partners, and the seller of the property. I knew he'd taken a big chance. I am one-hundred-percent sure he would have capitalized on it if he'd been able to. I should have asked. Maybe I could have helped."

"I wouldn't have told you, Luce," Liv answered honestly. "I never told a soul because … because I didn't want to let Michael down more than I already had."

"What are you talking about, Liv? You and Michael had the marriage everyone dreams of. I mean, I know you were both human—and nothing is perfect—but seriously, Liv."

"We let each other down in a million small ways. I mean who doesn't? Right? I couldn't let anybody know he'd taken that big of a loan—that he'd left us strapped for money. I couldn't let Bella know that she couldn't go to U of M because he died before he could make good on an investment. I just couldn't." Liv paused, her head shaking with her eyes closed. "A lot of good that did me, using some of my advance to pay for Bella's tuition. Goodness gracious. What a mess." Liv's sigh was heavy.

"There's no way to come up with a book by September?" Lucy asked.

"There is no way I can come up with a romance novel by September. I still can't write—" Liv's words cut off. She could write. She had written even more this morning. But she wasn't writing what she was contracted to write.

"I'm sorry, Liv. I really am. I wish I'd known earlier, I could have helped refinance or … something."

"There was nothing you were going to do to fix this, Luce. Nothing. I wouldn't have allowed it. Paying my bills is not your responsibility."

"No, I know that. But I can't help but think we could have helped. At the very least you wouldn't have had to shoulder all this on your own." Lucy smiled, a gentle sloping smile that indicated love and care. "Although, if I had to guess, I would say that Frannie knew about this?"

Liv laughed out loud. Frannie. No good at lying and no good at hiding it. "Just recently, I had to tell her. She's working on the house to get it ready to sell ..."

Lucy nodded her head. "She's been acting like a cat on a hot tin roof for weeks. I knew something was up. Listen, I know you're mad at Maggie," Lucy started, "but maybe what we all learned here is that despite best intentions, secrets aren't really for keeping from the Ladies of the Round Table."

Liv tipped her head up to the sky. It was a deep periwinkle blue today, with the fluffiest of white clouds drifting by. A *picture-perfect* summer day. "You are right. I mean, I want to be mad at Maggie. It's a little easier than being mad at myself. For goodness sakes, my husband dies and leaves us financially strapped, and instead of working my tail off to get us out of it I just ... can't. And to make matters worse ... how does one just completely not know their daughter *failed out of college?*"

"She's nearly an adult, Liv. She's going to make mistakes. We know this, we've done it. We made mistakes, kept secrets from our parents. We did it all. Remember when we snuck out in the middle of the night sophomore year and went skinny dipping at Harmony Beach?"

Liv laughed.

"It's not different for Bella. It's not different for you. Just because you're the parent now doesn't mean *your* kid isn't going to screw up. This won't even be the last time."

"Ugh. Do not say that out loud!" Liv drew out her words in a dramatic fashion. "I mean just this summer alone, I found her drunk on the back porch and she failed out of college."

"You know it's true, Liv. She's nineteen. Shoot—we're all just people trying to make our way and messing it up along the way."

"I know, you're right. I should text Maggie—"

"And Frannie," Lucy added.

"And Bella." Liv smiled. "The list of apologies and amends is long, it seems."

"No apology necessary here, my friend." Lucy wrapped Liv in a side hug as they sat side-by-side on the park bench. The branches of the weeping willow were nearly sweeping the ground, keeping time with the gentle breeze. The sun peeked through the lacy pattern of leaves, spilling warmth across the two women. "At the risk of talking about business—do you want me to come by next week so we can gather some information and make some decisions about the house? I can give you some comps and a potential listing price. Maybe we can look at refinancing?"

"I appreciate that, but I did look into refinancing. It won't work since I don't actually have an *income* and haven't had one for a few years. I don't think my book sales are bringing in enough to support us, I'm no longer relevant. But I would like you to come by and help me get it ready to list," Liv answered quietly.

"You got it." Lucy looked at her watch. "Shoot, Liv. I have that showing up in Franklin in forty-five minutes. Give me a minute to make a call or two, and I'll cancel—"

"Absolutely not. I'm fine. I'm going to sit here and make a few phone calls and get ready to go home and deal with my college drop-out. You go! Go to work." Liv smiled a weary, but resolved, turn of her lips.

"You sure?"

"I'm positive. Go sell a house."

Lucy hugged Liv one more time and walked back toward The Local Cup where her car was parked. Liv took a deep breath, looking up at the canopy of the huge tree she was sitting under. She had imagined that telling her friends the truth would be awful, but here in the safety of her friendship with Lucy, she realized that the truth was the only way that worked. She would have thought she learned that by now. Closing her eyes and resting her head back on the bench, the moments of warm sunshine gave her a respite from her reality. She pulled her arms around her chest, hugging her small frame, and took a deep breath.

Do the next right thing, Liv.

The words didn't pop into her mind, they were simply there. Like a constellation of stars in the daylight. She'd needed the darkness to see them again. It was something Michael used to say and a motto she relied on in the days right after Michael died. She'd forgotten it somehow, or at least forgotten to employ it. So now, she pulled out her phone and stared at the screen. And did the next right thing.

Chapter 21

Liv sent a message to Maggie and one to Frannie apologizing for running out on the Ladies meeting, and both answered with lots of love and forgiveness. Maggie apologized profusely for not telling Liv as soon as she knew Bella was in trouble—to which Liv conceded that Maggie was right to encourage Bella to tell her the truth. This really was between Liv and Bella, and Liv would be crazy not to be grateful that Bella had someone to talk to—since she wasn't talking to her.

Now all that was left to deal with today was Bella. Bella, her star athlete, uber-smart daughter who just failed out of college. Before heading home, Liv took a walk through town—much slower than her running pace from earlier—down past the amphitheater and out toward the docks. It was only one o'clock in the afternoon, and Bella wouldn't be done at Blooms until six. She needed some time to process what she'd learned and figure out how to approach Bella.

"One scoop of mint chocolate chip, please?" Liv

asked the young man behind the counter at Blue Moon Ice Cream Company. A few minutes later, Liv walked out toward the water, ice cream in hand. She'd spent countless hours on these docks as a teenager. She had worked at the fuel dock—where she met Josh. She had been nervous since she knew virtually nothing about boats or boating, let alone fueling them up or pumping them out. But a summer job where she spent her days in the sun on the water sounded perfect, so she'd learned on the go. She learned how to gas boats up, tie lines, pump them out (not a favorite job!), and carried blocks of ice and bags of snacks and drinks back to the boats. Her skin had been golden brown—probably the reason she had age spots on her chest and forehead now. Still, she wouldn't change it. For a moment the memories that filled her mind left her remembering a life that was simple back then, except it wasn't. The summer Liv's parents announced their divorce had been perhaps one of the most disruptive and stressful times of her life.

She was frustrated with Bella and disappointed for her—and truth be told, in her. But the longer Liv mulled the news of her daughter's grades around in her mind, the more she understood her daughter's behavior. It never feels good to let down the people you love. And not only did Bella fail out, she'd done so at her dad's alma mater and lost the scholarship her father had dreamt of. Big weight for a tiny girl.

Liv closed her eyes and swallowed a bit of ice cream off her spoon. The sharp taste of mint felt refreshing and nostalgic. When she opened them, she saw him in the distance.

He knelt down easily, washing down the sides of a boat—a thirty-two-foot Sea Ray, if she hadn't lost her touch. Déjà vu settled down like an early morning fog. Seeing Josh on his boat felt like déjà vu, but not in the traditional sense. No, seeing Josh was being reminded of who she used to be before life twisted her up and turned her back around. She could see a shadow of her younger self just by looking at him. She could see younger Olivia, the one with the world at her feet. She scraped the last bit of ice cream out of her dish, turning the spoon upside down in her mouth and savoring every drop. It was so easy to romanticize the past, to forget the weight of who you were and what you didn't know.

Suddenly, Josh caught sight of her. Standing to his full height, he stretched up and back as he tossed the boat rag from hand to hand. Their eyes locked. It occurred to Olivia that she should be embarrassed. That she should quickly make up a reason for why she was standing here on the dock that she *knew* was home to his parents' slip. Of course, she hadn't known he'd be here, but she had known he might.

"Hey, Liv," he offered.

She took a few steps down the dock toward Josh. There it was, the déjà vu again. *Josh.* Their friendship had started on these docks. Liv smiled now at remembering him back then. A boy, in bare feet, shorts, and a backward baseball hat, waving to her with a beaming smile. Only now, that young boy was a man. A man with strong arms, kind eyes, and ... Liv shook her head to stop the thoughts rolling quickly into her mind.

"Hey there, sailor." She smiled. *Where did that come from?* Liv wondered.

"How are you?" he asked as he deftly walked toward Liv and sat at the end of the boat. A leg straddled each side of the bow as he sat, arms draped over the steel rails, smiling at her.

"Umm ... I'm ... okay." She shrugged her shoulders. "I've had harder days, although this one isn't the best either. What are you up to?"

"I was just cleaning up the boat. My parents had it up at the dry docks, but still had their slip paid for. So since I decided to stay for a few more weeks—"

"You are?" Liv asked with more interest in her voice than she would have liked to give away.

"Working remotely. Benefit of being my own

show." Josh lifted his shoulders.

"That's nice." Liv felt a touch of ... jealousy? It wasn't just that she needed to write to save her career—if that was possible at all—it was also that she loved to work, to be productive and contribute. It felt oddly freeing and sad today, to have given up hope on her series, to have left the pressure of completing the book (or even starting it) and let go of the anchor her writer's block had tied to her waist. She'd stopped fighting. There was freedom in not being in limbo any longer. Still, she wished she had somewhere to be and something to do in the middle of the afternoon. And the reality was, she would have to figure something out regardless of the outcome of her writing career. She needed a job, and hearing about Josh working only served to drive that home.

"You know, I was just going to go out for a little cruise over to Anchor Bay. You want to come?"

Liv consulted her watch. She absolutely had to be home when Bella returned from work—but it was just about two o'clock, and Blooms didn't close until six. "Umm ..."

"We won't be gone long, I just wanted to get out in the sunshine for a bit."

She looked down at her clothes—a pair of cut-off jean shorts, a tank top, and flip-flops. It almost looked as if she'd dressed for a boat ride today. "You know what? Sure. Yeah. I have to be back home by six. Is that okay?"

"No problem at all." Josh easily shifted from his seated position up to standing and worked his way around to help Liv board.

Liv threw her ice cream cup in the trash and walked around to meet Josh at the side of the boat. He reached down and met her, squeezing her small hand inside his large one. His skin was warm and weathered against her own. That's when she felt it. *Heat.* The kind of heat she'd only felt for Michael in nearly thirty years. The kind of heat that traveled from her belly up into her chest, making her nervous and excited all at once. The kind of heat that told her she might be in trouble.

Chapter 22

"Is there anything that feels better than sunshine on your shoulders?" Josh asked. Liv smiled back at him, her short hair blowing as they scooted across the water. She was wearing an old pair of his sunglasses, Ray-Bans, he'd had stuffed in the back of the glove box. She hadn't had hers, so she'd borrowed his. He shook his head. He was acting like a teenager who was excited that the girl he liked was wearing his letterman jacket.

It's no big deal, he told himself. He knew Liv was still grieving her husband. And he had no intention of interfering with that or pushing her in any way. Still, he couldn't help the smile on his face. The ride out to Anchor Bay wouldn't be long. Liv sat shotgun, hanging on to the post next to her and looking around eagerly.

"Do you get out here much? I mean, on the water?" Josh asked, his voice just loud enough to be heard over the noise of the engine and wake.

"You know, I don't. For somebody who lives *on* the

lake, I spend embarrassingly little time *in* the lake! Michael wasn't much of a boater. He really enjoyed the view and being close to the water but …" Liv paused.

Josh waited for her to continue, hoping she would. It might sound crazy to some, but he was curious about her husband. She was a woman who knew and understood commitment. Every detail she gave him about Michael was fitting another puzzle piece into the years that had passed since he'd seen her last. Knowing a little more about Michael felt like he was getting to know Liv *now* a little better.

"Michael's cousin died in a drowning accident when he was young. They were best friends, he and Billy. Michael was eight, and Billy was six. I'm not sure of all the details—Michael wasn't either. Even though he'd been there when it happened, he was so young, the how of it all was beyond him. He always wanted to be near the water, and he loved our view. But he never had any interest in boating or being …" Liv looked around and swept her hand across the view. "Out here."

"That's awful. A life-changing event for certain." He kept his words few, choosing not to add or sympathize with Liv's story about Michael too much. Instead, he just wanted to listen.

The sluicing of the waves against the hull of the boat slowed as they pulled into the outer edges of Anchor Bay.

"You up to anchor for a little bit?" Josh asked. It was a fine line to respect her position—she still wore her wedding rings, so she was clearly still married in her mind—and to enjoy time with her himself. Josh wasn't sure if he was doing it right or not—he'd never dated a widow before. Not that this was dating. It was … Josh wasn't sure what it *was*, but he was having a distinct realization of what he *wanted* it to be.

"I'm up for whatever," Liv answered, and Josh smiled in return.

"You remember what to do to anchor?" he asked.

"Maybe? I might need a little direction. It's been … a while."

Josh gave easy and clear directions, and Liv was a quick study. He'd chosen a spot away from the other boats that had anchored there, not only for a little privacy but also to give them a wide berth to anchor. Turns out, they hadn't needed it.

Once the boat had tightened on a solid anchor, Josh and Liv sat together at the table on the back of the boat. Josh handed Liv a beer and grabbed one for himself. Liv tipped her face back toward the sun. Josh smiled. Watching Liv relax made him happy. And proud in an odd way. He knew Liv had been through a lot and was still struggling. To offer her an afternoon of sunshine and summertime felt good.

"So, how is Bella?" he asked.

Liv, still looking as if she was a melting pad of butter under the sun, let loose a rumble that turned to laughter deep in her throat. "That is a loaded question today."

Josh laughed, "I know the feeling. Somedays are harder than others."

"Yes. They are."

Josh waited for Liv to say more, and when she didn't, he chose not to press it.

"How are your kids?" Liv asked.

"Lacy is good. She just finished her third year of college at Ohio State, but she's a senior in credits. She'll be done in one more semester. Wants to head to law school. I have no doubt that will happen. She's always been driven, focused, and ambitious. Zane, on the other hand, he's my wanderer. He's at a small school in Virginia. I don't think he'll go back. He did just finish his third year, but he only has enough credits to be a sophomore. He's working a demolition-construction job this summer, and you know what? He loves it. School is just—he's like a square peg trying to fit into a round hole, ya know?"

Liv nodded.

"Dina keeps pressuring him. It hasn't gone well, in fact … well, she's pushed him away, to be honest. It's hard for her that he doesn't want to go to college. Mostly because she doesn't want to tell people that he's 'just working' and not in school. It's been a fight. He hasn't spoken to his mom in three months." Josh tried to temper his words, which was sometimes hard when it came to his ex-wife. His children never heard him speak ill of her, and they never would. But the way she had been treating Zane as if he was less than because he wasn't living her expected path, well, that was a deal-breaker. He wouldn't let his son feel bad about an honest wage.

Still, it was interesting, Josh thought. How Liv had lost Michael in a cruel twist of fate and Josh and Dina had fallen apart, willingly in the end. It occurred to him now that his attraction to Liv—which was growing by the minute—wasn't just attraction or nostalgia for a summer love. It was more than that. It was a desire, deep in Josh's heart, to be loved in the same way Liv loved Michael. Dina had never loved him the way Liv loved Michael. And Josh had never realized how much that mattered to him until now. It wasn't that he wanted to *be Michael* or replace Michael, as much as he had discovered he was attracted to the kind of woman who loved deeply. And that was Liv. It had finally dawned on him that he wanted to be on the receiving end of that kind of devotion. The devotion Liv was capable of giving.

Liv's cheeks turned pink, and she turned her head to look out at the lake. Josh wondered what he'd said. Had he spoken too harshly about Dina? Would that be difficult for Liv to hear? Before he had too much time to wonder or course correct, Liv spoke.

"How did you and Dina meet?"

"Funny, we met in college. Just a few weeks after I left here. A few weeks after that summer." Josh looked at her. He tried to keep his eyes from giving way the intensity of the connection he felt with this woman. He wasn't one to believe that things happen for a reason—Justin's death was proof of that, and he assumed Liv felt the same way about Michael being taken so early. But what he did feel when he was with Liv was a continuation of their story.

They had fallen in love as teenagers. It's true that young love doesn't often last, and it's so easy to romanticize something that didn't come to be. And even more, Bella, Lacy, and Zane wouldn't be here if Josh and Liv had stayed their course, which was reason enough to be grateful their romance ended when it did. But given where they were now, and that the relationships they'd started after they broke up were the only ones standing between then and now, Josh couldn't help but wonder if the universe was trying to tell him something. Well, the universe and his undeniable attraction to this small but strong woman.

"We didn't actually start dating until our senior year of college, and then we just kind of … fell into marriage. I think I told you before, we just did the next thing on the list, and neither of us thought about it much, I don't think."

Josh stood up to grab two more beers and a small container filled with cheese and crackers. "We weren't miserable while we were married—at least I wasn't. We just weren't … great." He laughed again. "In fact, we weren't even good. But I was building my company, and we were raising the twins. Life was busy, and to be honest, I don't think I would have ever left. I was really focused on the business and—I'm embarrassed to admit—living in an essentially loveless marriage felt okay to me because I didn't really want to deal with what it would take to fix it or end it. In many ways I'm grateful to Dina for having the guts to walk out."

"So you are happier now?" Liv asked, reaching for a cracker and brushing hands with Josh. Josh felt an electric jolt shoot through him. It wasn't as if he hadn't touched Liv before. In fact, they'd held hands just today when he helped hoist her up onto the boat. But this unintentional, everyday, normal brushing of hands felt different. Almost as if their touching—over crackers—was the highlighted passage in a book. The part that was important.

Josh cleared his throat and took a swig of his beer. "I am happier now. I mean, I missed having my kids with me all the time and I carried a lot of guilt over disrupting their childhood. I really do owe her the happiness I've found over the past few years. And ironically, the relationships I have with my kids are much stronger now than they were, or would have been, had we stayed together. That definitely makes me happy. So, yeah. I'm good."

"That summer when my parents divorced was so hard for me. I always wondered why it hit so hard. I mean, they spent most of their time fighting as it was so I'm not sure what my sixteen-year-old heart wanted them to stay together for. I wish I could say I was closer to them each because of it or that they were kinder to each other after. But they weren't. Really, in some ways they were worse."

"My parents were rock solid until my dad died. I never worried, never didn't *just know* that they would be there, together. My kids didn't have that. After the divorce, Dina and I were at odds over everything at first. I think it's played a lot into who my kids are.

Lacey, the overachiever. Zane, the lost soul. Both handling not having a predictable home life in different ways. I thought about you during that time. How your parents' divorce affected you. Years before I did it to my kids, you gave me a window into what it felt like to have that happen *to* you. I was always oddly grateful for that. Not that I am happy it happened to you or to Dina and me, but I was grateful to *know* how hard it was. I handled the kids differently because of it. I worked harder at my relationship with my kids because of you."

Josh closed his eyes and nodded a thank you in her direction. Taking his last sip of beer and reaching for a bottle of water, he watched as Liv curled her feet up under her, sitting crisscross applesauce in her seat. She tucked a lock of hair behind her ear and took a deep breath.

He wondered if what he'd just said—that he hadn't had just random passing thoughts of her over the years—was too much. He watched closely to see if he'd frightened her or made her uncomfortable. He hoped he hadn't—it wasn't his intent. He'd always wanted to thank her for sharing that part of her life with him. And now he had.

"Tell me about Michael," Josh said.

Liv looked at Josh and then her wrist. She spun her

watch around in circles. "Michael and I were together most of our lives. Outside of the summer I spent ... with you—" Liv paused to clear her throat. Josh could hear the emotion thick in her words, giving them heft. He thought about telling her she didn't need to tell him anything she didn't want to, but then he looked in her eyes and saw a teaspoon of relief. As if telling someone the tale of Michael and Liv who didn't know about Michael and Liv was exactly what she needed.

"That summer Michael was studying abroad. In London. We had been together just six months, maybe less. I was only sixteen, nearly seventeen when he left. He wanted to go to London unencumbered. He didn't want to worry about a girlfriend. So, he broke up with me." Liv took a deep breath and then a sip of her beer. She closed her eyes for just a moment and opened them again.

Josh followed her gaze toward the sparkling view. The sunshine bounced off the water as if someone had thrown diamonds across the horizon. There were a few boats anchored around them, but none close enough to hear. Liv and Josh were in their own world. Floating, aimlessly, with no agenda and no plan. It felt good. It felt right. It felt familiar. Josh hoped Liv felt the same.

She continued, "When he came home, you'd been gone a few weeks. And I had started school. I remember going to pick him up at the airport. He'd called his parents—you know, back before cell phones—and asked them to bring me with them to pick him up. So, I went. We never broke up again."

"Were you happy?" Josh asked.

Liv's eyes pooled with tears. "We *were* happy. We had a good—no, we had a *great* marriage. Right until the end."

"I'm so glad," Josh answered, taking her hand in his. He gave it a quick squeeze before he let it go.

"I mean, we weren't perfect—"

"Nobody is," he added with a shake of his head.

"No, nobody is. But we were good to each other and loved each other. He was my very best friend—I suppose that is what hurts the most. Losing my best friend. I was the second half of a whole for so long. All of my adult life. In the beginning, and still sometimes now, it felt a little like I am walking around without … myself. If that makes any sense at all." She gave a self-deprecating laugh.

"I won't even comment. I have no idea. I think however it feels and however you describe it only has to make sense to you. I'm so sorry you had to go through that, that you are *going* through that."

"Me, too." Her eyes sparkled with tears, matching the glistening water out over the bow of the boat.

"Have you been writing?"

Liv fiddled with the label on her beer, pulling it off in small pieces. "I have been trying."

"So, I downloaded one of your books this past week," Josh said with a smirk.

"You did? Which one?" Liv laughed, her eyes suddenly taking on a sheen of joy instead of sadness.

"*January in Winter Springs*," Josh said the title of her first novel as if he were the audio actor doing a voice-over.

Liv laughed again. "I'm not sure it's your cup of tea."

"I already finished it! Who doesn't love a story about a woman falling back in love with her long-lost high school sweetheart?" Josh's lips curled up on either side.

"Right? Who doesn't love that?" Liv answered.

"You ready to go home?" Josh asked.

"Actually, I am," Liv stood up and helped Josh pack away their small picnic, then pull the anchor.

When they took off, Josh squeezed the back of Liv's neck as she sat next to him. He had half expected her to flinch—she was a woman in love with her husband, regardless if he was here to love or not. But she hadn't. Josh settled into the rhythm of the water, wondering how on earth he would keep this avalanche of feelings for the first love of his life at bay.

Chapter 23

"I cannot believe Maggie told you." Bella was furious. Her words spit out at Liv like darts coming in toward a board.

"Don't be mad at Maggie, Bella. She was only doing what she thought was right. You put her in a really bad position when you asked her to keep a secret from me." Liv worked hard to keep her voice steady and in control. "I am really grateful you have her to talk to, but *you* should have told me."

"You, you, you … that's all I ever hear from you is what I didn't do right. What I'm not doing right. What I need to do. Just stop. Okay? I don't want to hear any of it." Bella stormed into the living room and out onto the porch. Liv followed her daughter. She knew this conversation would not be easy, but she hadn't anticipated the level of difficulty would top ten.

"Bella. This is on you. Not on anyone else."

"I realize that, Mom. Don't you think I know that? I'm the one who messed up. I'm the one who failed out. I am the one who did it all wrong. I get it. I'm not good enough and I never will be."

At that Liv's head spun around quickly. "What are you talking about, Bella?" she asked, her voice quiet. She had said those exact words to her own mother at her age. Had Liv done to Bella what Liv's mom had done to her? Oh God, she hoped not.

"Did anyone ever stop and ask *me* if I wanted to go to U of M? Did anyone ever stop and ask *me* if I even wanted to go to college?" Bella's face was red, her eyes brimmed with tears, threatening to disrupt her nearly uncontrolled emotions.

Liv started to answer, but Bella interrupted immediately. "Let me answer that for you. No. You didn't. You never, ever asked me. You just assumed. I hated U of M, Mom! I hated it. And I hated college."

"Why didn't you tell me that, Bella? It's not like I signed the papers or I made the decision—you decided. You did. And I never *once* heard that you didn't want to go."

"I couldn't tell you that." Bella's tears now fell with abandon. "I couldn't tell you the one thing you looked forward to every day, the one thing you wanted more than anything, the one thing that kept you going after Daddy died was me going to college. Me getting a scholarship. I couldn't tell you. I just couldn't."

"Oh, Bella." Liv's voice was barely a whisper. She sat down, defeated, in the old wicker rocker and put her head in her hand as she rocked back and forth. Missing Michael at this moment came like a heavy boulder on her chest. Her eyes filled with tears. Michael tears. The kind that came in fast and furious, like a storm off the lake.

"I couldn't do that to you and I couldn't do that to Daddy. But I also couldn't do school. I just couldn't. At first I thought it was going to be great, ya know? Nobody knew about Dad. Nobody knew you were a writer. I could just be … me. Bella. And then I started to fall behind. I admit—I went out too much and I started to skip class, but it wouldn't have mattered. It was all way above my head and I was so far behind I … I just couldn't do it."

"Bella, come sit here, will you?" Liv patted the matching rocker next to her. Hearing the wood floor squeak under her with each rhythmic tip of the chair helped to calm Liv, slow down her thoughts. How had she missed all of this? How had she gotten so far off track with her daughter? Her own mother had been focused on success. She'd expected excellence out of everything Liv did. She'd hated living under the impending doom if she didn't live up to her mother's expectations, and she hated withstanding her mom's critiques of every little thing she did. She had tried hard—so hard—with Bella not to repeat that. Clearly, she'd missed the mark.

Suddenly Liv thought of Josh. Well, not Josh exactly. But his ex-wife, Dina. She didn't want to have anything in common with Josh's ex-wife. The woman he wasn't truly happy with. The woman who left him. The one who didn't allow her son to chart his own course. It had been easy to condemn her in her mind earlier on the boat, but now, sitting here with her daughter, her own mistakes were glaring. The feelings of embarrassment she'd felt since she had read Bella's report card smoldered from a leaping flame to the smallest ember. She shouldn't be embarrassed Bella failed out of school. And she should be embarrassed that she didn't *know* that Bella was struggling, and that she didn't know *why*.

Bella walked toward Liv in an arc away from the chair. As if walking a few feet away could buffer her from an oncoming attack. There was a part of Liv that wanted to scream, "Failing out of school was *not* okay and lying about it was downright *wrong*!" *But,* if she had wrongly imitated her mom's critical ways—and it appeared she had—she would have to take a one-hundred-and-eighty-degree turn away from them to save her relationship with Bella. Liv had to set aside being angry ... and listen.

Liv picked up her phone and looked at it. "I talked to Coach Cooper. He was really worried about you. In fact, he said he left me a message a few weeks ago. I never got it ..." Liv let her voice trail off at the end. She didn't want to accuse Bella of anything, but she was pretty sure she knew what happened to the message. And while she was trying to do things differently, she also still believed the only way through this mess was ... honesty.

"Yeah. About that." Bella told her mom how she'd deleted the message and missed call so she wouldn't know. Liv nodded and held her hands clasped together in her lap. Her palms were sweaty, and her heart was beating with anxiety. She focused on her daughter, on looking into her eyes. She'd reached out once to touch Bella's knee and she had recoiled. Just a touch, but enough that Liv knew there was a lot of work to be done.

"He called again tonight, just before you got home actually. I wish I had known earlier how much you were struggling. Why didn't you tell me, Bella? Why didn't you tell me when you got home how much trouble you were in?"

"I was going to. I really was. I was going to tell you after the Summer Kickoff Festival, but then I overheard you telling Mrs. Hollingsworth at the fireworks how good I was doing at school and with track. I just couldn't let you down. And then there was the whole Tequila Night mess …"

"But Bella, erasing messages off of my phone? Throwing away your grade report? You even lied about having breakfast with Hannah. Sweet pea … that's not okay."

"I know it's not … I just … I just didn't know what to do. And I was going to text Hannah, I was. I just couldn't. I was so excited to come home. I was so relieved. And then I got here, and everything was all different."

"Different? Sweet pea, not much has changed. Not even the leaky faucet in the kitchen. I mean, Frannie fixed it, and the leak is back!" Liv tried for a little levity, hoping to get Bella to smile.

"I think in my mind, when I came home … I don't know. It was all weird with Hannah when I left for school. I was trying to make new friends and she stayed here at home. It was weird. I really wanted to come home and have everything back to … normal. But when I got here, everything was different …" Bella's voice faded to black.

"You miss Dad," Liv said. The realization came to her as quickly as if she had never connected Bella's troubles with missing her father, or her own writer's block with Michael's death. Of course she had, she just didn't know what to do about it. She couldn't bring Michael back. So how did she solve the problem?

"I miss him so much, Mom. I do." Bella cried now in earnest, her shoulders shaking under the weight of grief and failure. "It's like there is nothing of him here. His shoes aren't by the door and his car isn't in the driveway and his clothes aren't in his closet."

And that is when Liv knew what to do. She rubbed her daughter's back until her cries settled from a raging storm to a gentle rain, and then she left.

Chapter 24

Managing the small doorway onto the porch with the large cardboard box was cumbersome, but Liv passed through without much trouble. Bella sat with her legs bent up, hugging them to her chest. She wiped her tears on her knees as Liv sat down beside her.

"The lake is pretty tonight," Bella said. "I love when the sun goes down and the water turns that purple-y color."

"Me too," Liv said. She looked around the porch, taking in the matchstick ceiling, the old painted floorboards, the stacked row of windows facing the water and wrapping around each side to showcase the fresh coastline. She looked at the old wicker furniture she and Michael had redone, painted a sky blue with yellow cushions. How she loved this house. Her heart hurt knowing that although she was trying to rebuild a bridge between her and her daughter, she would burn it all again when Bella found out they had to sell the only place she had ever called home.

On the way home from Josh's boat, she'd decided she would tell Bella about the house tonight. Get all the cards on the table. Bella's grades, losing her scholarship, Liv's advance and the house. All of it. But it was clear, after the conversation they just had, that telling Bella about the house tonight would not be wise. No, she would have to wait a little longer. Tonight, they had something else to do.

"Hey, do you see that freighter?" Bella pointed out toward the south end of the view. "It's always amazing how huge those ships are and how small they look from here. I didn't even see it until just now."

"Oh, I do see it. Your dad and I always used to wonder how long they would be on the horizon before we noticed them. It's like you look up and all a sudden, there they are. Right in front of you where you'd been looking all the time."

"Dad loved the freighters, didn't he?" Bella's voice quivered with memory.

Liv smiled and closed her eyes. "He sure did, Bella. He did." Rummaging through the box in front of her, she found exactly what she was looking for. "He also loved this flannel." Liv handed Bella Michael's well-worn red buffalo pattern flannel to her daughter. "He wore this the day before he died. It was in the laundry basket—well, actually …" Liv laughed. "It was on the floor next to the laundry basket. He was a terrible shot."

Bella took the shirt into her hands, rubbing the softly worn fabric against her wet cheeks. A small cry echoed between them.

"I can still smell him, I think, if I close my eyes and try really hard," Liv said.

Bella followed her mom's advice, sinking her face deep into her daddy's shirt, pulling air and life into her lungs. She nodded her head yes, the words too tough to utter.

"I also saved you his favorite Detroit Tigers T-shirt. And this, his favorite U of M sweatshirt." Liv began piling the saved pieces of Michael on her daughter's lap. "And here, his favorite blanket he used to curl up with and watch TV—and freighters!"

Liv and Bella spent the next hour going through the box of Michael's belongings. Taking turns crying, and sometimes crying together. When they got to the bottom of the box Bella took a deep breath. "I wish there was more."

Liv's stomach clenched. There was more, one box. But that box was hers. There was a part of Liv and Michael that had been only Liv-and-Michael, not Liv-and-Michael-and-Bella. She'd told Josh she missed her best friend, and that was true. She missed the secrets they had, the pieces of each other that only they knew. The whispered conversations under the cover deep in the night. Talking about their dreams over coffee early in the morning. That box—*her* box—was for her and only her.

"I suppose I should have waited for you to come home to go through his things. I'm sorry, Bella. I could have handled that better. It just took me so long to do it at all—he'd been gone a year and a half before I even started. Once I had the courage, I just did it. But this box, this box is for you. Everything in it. You can keep."

"Don't you want any of it, Mom?" The words were nearly accusatory.

"I have my own memories, Bella. I have a few mementos I kept of my own. I picked these ones for you, especially."

"Oh, okay," she answered, some of the edge in her voice gone.

They had bridged such a gap tonight, Liv was a little taken back by Bella's suddenly cool temperature. Instead of brushing it under the table, or assuming she understood, she decided to ask. "Bella, what's wrong?"

"I just don't want anybody to forget him," she said, her eyes unable to meet her mother's gaze.

"Are you afraid I'm going to forget your dad?" Liv

said, her voice unable to hide the shock.

"Well, you can replace him. I can't. I'll never, ever have another dad. But you ... you could have another husband."

Liv leaned back in her chair. *Where did that come from?* she wondered. In the two years since Michael had passed, Liv had not had more than a passing conversation with another man—until Josh. And Bella didn't know a thing about him—except Tequila Night. Ahhh, yet another thing Liv screwed up. She should have known. "There are not a lot of things I know for certain, Bella. One of the things I know is that until my dying day, until the very last breath that passes my lips, I will never, ever forget your dad. Ever."

"Does that mean you won't ever get remarried?" Bella asked.

The question took Liv by surprise. She had expected to talk about Bella's grades tonight, and if she was honest, she knew they would talk about Michael. She did *not* know she would be discussing a future love life with her daughter. Liv tucked her hair behind her ear and tipped her head upwards. She shivered a bit. The sun had gone down, and the porch was now fully in the dark outside of the few lights they'd turned on as they talked. Wrapping her arms around her legs, she realized that if Bella had asked her that question even a month ago, she would have had a different answer than tonight.

"Bella, if there is one thing your father's death has taught me, it is quite simply that I can try as hard as I want, but I can't predict what will happen. I'm not planning on getting remarried, but I wasn't planning on being a widow, either. The only thing I *know* is that my love for your dad and my love for you is as endless as the view across the lake.

"The morning your dad died we sat out on this porch and had coffee. We watched the sun come up together." Liv waited for her voice to waver. But it didn't. Inside her was a rising strength. "As I remember it, the sunrise was beautiful. It was one of those mornings where the fog mixes with the clouds, and as the sun rises you can't tell the difference between the heavens and the water. That's how I see my love for your dad—and you. Heaven or Earth, it's with me. Always. I can't tell the difference between loving your dad here or loving your dad … up there. I don't know if I'll ever get married again. I only know if I do, it will be because I have enough space in my heart to love two men. Because your dad, he's not going anywhere."

With that, Bella laid her head on Liv's shoulder and wrapped the two of them up underneath Michael's favorite blanket, together.

Chapter 25

"These blueberries look delicious!" Lucy pulled on Liv's sleeve and tugged her over to the stall where a local farmer had a table full with quarts of plump, deep blue berries. Liv and Lucy both bought two quarts apiece and added them to their collection of goodies from the downtown farmer's market. The fourth of July weekend was Liv's favorite of the year, summer was in full bloom. The weather was hot and the dog days of summer still stretched out in front of them without a hint of an end. July fourth was the summer's Saturday—full of fun with the fall so far off it wasn't of any concern.

Liv and Lucy were having a halfsies meeting of the Ladies of the Round Table. Maggie had canceled last minute because of an emergency with the boys, and Frannie had gone to Georgia to spend the holiday with her parents and Mamaw Dixie–Frannie's favorite person on Earth. Even without their crew of four, the two friends decided to go ahead with their afternoon, starting with mimosas and brunch at The Local Cup and moving on to the farmer's market in downtown Blue Water Bay. The weekly market was larger than normal, hosting plenty of visiting vendors to celebrate the biggest summer holiday weekend. The street was closed down the entire length of town with booths of fresh fruit, veggies, kettle corn, potted plants, homemade pasta, handmade gifts and trinkets, a smoothie stand, and a hot dog cart. The air was thick with the smell of deep battered fish at the end of the street where the annual Lions Club perch fish fry had a line out the tent and around the corner.

"Don't look now, but Angela is over by the popcorn stand." Lucy laughed. "Who wears stilettos to a farmer's market? I don't even get it. She absolutely does not understand reading your audience."

Liv turned her head just a little to the south, on reflex more than curiosity. She saw Angela talking, her hands flailing wildly around as she told a story to ... to Josh. Liv felt a hot poker of ... jealousy? ... sear through her belly. *Jealousy?* No, it couldn't be. She had no right and no reason to be jealous of Angela talking to Joshua Hart. None at all. Still, she couldn't deny that nagging feeling that pulled around the sides of her heart.

"Wait, is that Josh?" Lucy leaned across Liv in an effort to catch a glimpse of Angela's target. "I can't tell for sure. I have only seen him once since we ran into him at the Summer Kickoff."

"Yes, that's him," Liv answered with her best effort at sounding … normal, but the gentle tremor in her voice was undeniable. She tried not to turn the rest of the way around, instead focusing on the homegrown honey at the next vendor she came to. She picked up a jar of the liquid gold and read the label, only to put it down and pick up another.

"Spill it, Liv," Lucy said.

"Spill what? There is nothing to spill!" Liv's voice lilted upward just enough to completely betray her words.

"Oh really? Well, you have now picked up *three* identical bottles of honey and read their labels. Three, Liv. Three. Spill. It."

Startling as she realized she had, in fact, done that, Liv smiled at her friend as she put down the bottle of honey.

Lucy pulled her Maui Jim glasses down the length of her nose so that she could look Liv in the eye. "I wasn't around that summer, Liv, so I don't remember. But Josh does. Obviously. And if that isn't intriguing enough—which it is, by the way—you've mentioned him plenty lately. I know there is something to spill. So spill it, Olivia." Lucy smiled at her friend and readjusted her glasses.

"There is nothing to spill," Liv insisted. "We were friends as kids and have reconnected to be friends as adults. That's it." Liv's eyes slanted toward Angela and Josh again.

"Is that why you can't stop trying to watch Angela and Josh's conversation?" Lucy turned the full weight of her squared shoulders toward Josh and Angela.

"I'm not—" Liv started as she tried to gently turn Lucy back around without success.

"Just stop. You are. You are trying to watch them over your shoulder! I have a much clearer view and I can tell you right now that she's trying awfully hard and he's not paying that much attention. Actually, it looks like he has an older woman with him?"

With that Liv turned all the way around.

"Yes, you're right. You don't care at all." Lucy's smile leapt up from her lips to her eyes.

Liv tipped her head back toward the sky—the blue peeking through from under low slung clouds that were just dark enough to threaten rain. "Ugh," Liv answered her friend. "Just because I don't want to see him chatting up Angela doesn't mean I want him—"

Just as Liv was finishing her sentence, Lucy caught

Josh's eye and waved. "You are going to thank me for this," she said as she began walking in Josh's direction. Josh said goodbye to Angela and made his way toward Liv and Lucy.

"Hi there, Josh. How are you?" Lucy's full sales smile was on high.

"Nice to see you again." Josh smiled, his eyes darting from Lucy toward Liv nearly instantly.

Liv's stomach twisted in knots. How was it possible that she could feel like a teenager when she was a middle-aged widow? "Hi Josh, how are you?" Liv reached her hand out to shake Josh's just as he offered his arm for a small hug. Liv stepped awkwardly toward Josh and slipped gently into his embrace. His hand brushed her lower back as it passed through, and Liv's skin prickled with ... what? Excitement? Nervousness? She wasn't sure, but it felt an awful lot like what happened when their hands connected over crackers on the boat.

"I'm good." Josh turned toward the woman next to him. As he did so, their side profiles matched perfectly, and Liv recognized who the woman was. "Liv, you remember my mom, Dorothy?"

Josh finished introductions of Dorothy to Lucy, his raven-haired mom still stood tall despite her waning years. Liv remembered fondly the kind woman who had been generous with her time all those years ago when Liv had struggled through the summer of her parents' divorce. Waves of memories she'd long forgotten about soothed her, Mrs. Hart making chocolate chip cookies in the kitchen and inviting Liv to help. Mr. and Mrs. Hart taking Josh and Liv on a boat ride down to the Detroit River. Mrs. Hart working in her garden, pruning her bumper crop of rose bushes.

"It's so nice to see you again, Mrs. Hart." Liv smiled, reaching her hand out toward Dorothy.

"Oh my goodness, Olivia Harrison. Joshua told me he'd run into you a few weeks ago. It's wonderful to see you." Dorothy smiled, her blue eyes dancing with kindness, if not a tiny bit … vague. "Do you know I've read all of your books—and I didn't even know it was you! I loved every one."

The compliment from a woman who Liv had looked up to as a young girl felt warm and sweet, like pancake syrup dripping off her heart. The summer Josh and Liv had spent together had been marked not only with the end of her parents' marriage, but also with the challenges every teenage girl faces. Dorothy had made Liv welcome, she'd been kind, and she had helped Liv to see that there was so much in this world to be offered.

"Well, that just means the world to me. Thank you, so much," Liv offered.

"Have you two tried the perch yet?" Dorothy asked. "Would you like to join us? We were just headed over."

"No, we haven't," Lucy answered, turning toward Liv and then looking directly at Josh. "I would *love* to, but I actually have to go check in on a client in a few minutes."

Liv looked sideways at Lucy. She hadn't mentioned needing to work earlier.

"Liv, do you want to come along?" Josh asked. "I hear it's excellent. It sure smells good!"

"Go ahead, Liv," Lucy added. "I'm just going to go back to the car and make a few phone calls. I'll meet up with you in a bit."

"Oh, okay. Sure, that sounds good." Liv stumbled over her words as her friend disappeared into the crowd quicker than the baseball players into the corn in that famous baseball movie. And just like that, Liv was having lunch with Josh.

Chapter 26

Liv stared into her reflection in the mirror as she pondered the fourth bathing suit she had tried on in the last twenty minutes. Deciding between this one and bathing suit number one, the yellow one-piece, was proving to be quite difficult. What she really needed was someone else's opinion, which was also the very last thing she would ask for. While she had accepted Josh and Dorothy's invitation to go for a cruise down to the Detroit River this afternoon, she also wasn't up to talking about it. Not even with the Ladies of the Round Table.

Somehow, dropping by Josh's boat and unexpectedly going on an afternoon ride felt more acceptable than *accepting* an invitation from Josh and Dorothy to take a ride down to the Detroit River for the afternoon. This time felt more … important? Obvious? Purposeful? This time, there was time to prepare—and think. Overthink. *Was this a date?* She had no idea if it was a date or not. Her stomach flipped in knots—which was amazing in and of itself because she was busy clenching it as tightly as she could, trying to see herself the way she wanted to in the mirror. With a heaving sigh, she let out her sucked-in stomach and rounded her shoulders in defeat. *She shouldn't go. Nope. She shouldn't. She will just text Josh and tell him something came up.*

Just as Liv reached behind her back to unhook her black and white halter top, the door busted open behind her.

"Hey, Mom—" Bella started and stopped. "What are you doing?"

"Oh, just trying on some bathing suits," Liv answered as she quickly threw the shorts and T-shirt, sweatshirt, and towel she'd gathered into her large beach bag.

"Obviously ..." Bella drew out each syllable of the word as if she thought Liv could not hear her. "*Why* are you trying on bathing suits?"

Liv's brow beaded ever so gently with a sheen of sweat. Women going through perimenopause shouldn't have to deal with dating *or* teenage daughters in the middle of a hot flash. "It's July, Bella. July fourth weekend. In Michigan. Everyone wears a bathing suit." She was being vague, purposefully, and it obviously was doing nothing to throw Bella off the scent. In fact, Liv had probably just shown her hand.

"Very funny. Where are you *going* in a bathing

suit?"

Liv took a deep breath. A minute ago she thought she hadn't wanted to go. She'd wanted nothing more than to take off her bathing suit and crawl back into a comfy pair of shorts and a T-shirt and watch Netflix. Something far less frightening than getting on a boat with Josh Hart. On purpose. Like a date. But something about the way Bella surprised her exposed what she *really* wanted to do—which was go on a boat, on purpose, with Josh Hart. She wasn't doing a thing wrong. Nothing. Michael was gone, and Josh was her friend. He'd been her friend for over thirty years! There was no reason she couldn't go on a boat ride with her *friend*. Even if it was a date.

"A friend of mine invited me on a ride down to the Detroit River this afternoon. Our fireworks in town aren't until tomorrow night, so I thought it would be fun."

"What friend?" Bella crossed her arms and locked them into place. This girl could be fierce when she wanted. Her long brown ponytail curled just slightly over her shoulder, until she whipped it behind her.

"My friend Josh and his *mom*, Dorothy."

Bella continued to watch Liv as she skittered around the room picking up wayward clothes, straightening a corner of her bed, and packing and re-stacking the items in her bag. Bella stood stock still as she watched Liv pull on a casual pair of shorts and a tank top to cover up her suit.

"Do I know Josh?" Bella asked.

Liv took her time to answer, finally standing still and turning toward Bella. "Well, you met him the night of the Summer Kickoff Party—but I'm not sure you would remember." Liv hated to bring up Tequila Night, but the fact of the matter was that *is* when her daughter had met Josh and her daughter *may not* remember if she'd met him at all.

"Oh, so was he like the guy who carried me inside?"

"Yep. That's the one. Josh Hart. He's a nice man. He's back here this summer taking care of his mom, she's having some health issues—"

"Wait, back here?" Bella asked.

Liv stopped. She hadn't intended to fill Bella in on her and Josh's history. I mean, it wasn't necessarily Bella's business, and for certain it wouldn't help her cause for Bella to know they dated one sweet summer in high school when Bella's entire life she thought her parents had been together since … well, since the beginning.

"He was a summer kid. Back when I was in high school. His parents had a boat and cottage here in town. I worked the fuel docks, remember? So I met him then. Just randomly ran into him again at the Summer Kickoff." Liv was rambling. Too much information, and Bella was sure to be suspicious now.

"Did Dad know him?" Bella's arms stayed crossed across her chest.

"No, he didn't. He wasn't around much that summer." *Or at all,* Liv thought. "Listen, I've gotta go, sweet pea. I am meeting Dorothy and Josh down at the docks in thirty minutes and I don't want to be late. Did you need me for something?" Liv tossed her bag over her shoulder, hoping she'd remembered everything she might need. A lock of hair fell down in front of her eyes, and she flicked her head to the side to coax it out of the way, too afraid to move her hand to adjust it.

"Oh, I was just going to tell you I texted Hannah. I'm going to a beach bonfire with her tonight. She invited me." Bella's smile was small, but bright. And while Liv was excited that Bella was feeling included—she was also worried. Bella, at a beach bonfire, without Liv at home.

Liv's face gave away her concern. "Mom, don't worry. I won't repeat Tequila Night. Go, have fun on your boat ride with your *friend*." Bella smiled and turned and walked downstairs, leaving Liv holding a bag full of random summer belongings and a heart scared to death. She was going on a boat, on purpose.

Chapter 27

"Can you see that house there? Through the trees?" Dorothy asked as Josh skillfully navigated them along the shoreline toward the Detroit River.

"I think I can see the outline, yes?" Birch and pine trees clouded the clear view of the home that Dorothy was pointing to. The sun was playing peek-a-boo today between large, fluffy clouds that occasionally had a gray din, hinting at the potential for rain. The breeze was July-warm, and Liv couldn't help but close her eyes behind her sunglasses from time to time just to soak it in. Her nervousness at the prospect of a boat ride with Josh and Dorothy had settled to a gentle, exciting hum instead of the loud cacophony it was earlier.

"Rumor has it that the mistress to *someone* in the Ford family was kept there. Not against her will, of course ... but a kept woman just the same." Dorothy's eyes danced with the sunshine reflecting off of the water and also the excitement of such a story.

"Really? I never heard that!" *Hmmm,* Liv pondered.

How in the world had she never heard that story? Seeing the world from here, the water, gave Liv an entirely different perspective. She had always understood Michael's reluctance and fear of the water—but she also realized now that being *on* the water gave her solace and excitement.

"Oh yes, there is so much history here. Just around this bend of the coastline here, right up there." Dorothy pointed, leaning forward in her seat. "See those old buildings built right into the shore? There?" Dorothy turned toward Liv, clearly enjoying sharing the stories she knew.

"I think I do ... just parts of the foundation now? Is that what I'm looking for?"

"Yes. Those are the leftovers of bootlegger buildings. Detroit was big in rum-running. When the river froze over, bootleggers would fill their trucks with booze from Canada and drive right over the ice to the U.S.."

Liv looked closely at the remains of the structures, letting the subtle weight of a new muse settle on her shoulders. She recognized it right away, this inkling of curiosity, the small seedling of a new idea. *A historical romance? One set in prohibition times?* Liv worked her mind around to the present, not allowing it to slip into the what-ifs of plotting a story. She wanted to be here, in the moment, enjoying Dorothy and Josh. She wanted to collect details and nuggets of inspiration and allow them to simmer. Still, the excitement was there, deep in her soul. An *idea*. A *story*.

"Can you imagine?" Liv said, her gaze cast outward toward the water, choppy now with holiday weekend boat traffic. She smiled back at Dorothy and caught Josh's eyes just above his mother's. He smiled back, a smile nearly as familiar to her as her own, she realized. Even though the time they spent together had been marked by adolescence and the decades between with their own marriages, she couldn't help but realize the memory of his smile, the kindness of his eyes, and the gentle way in which he handled her tender sixteen-year-old heart had stayed with her. She'd hung on to his memory deep in her mind, and now here he was.

"It must have been exciting!" Dorothy added. "The crack of the ice underneath the truck, the frigid air. All for a little rum." She laughed.

"Speaking of rum!" Josh announced. "I made a Fourth of July Rum Punch for you ladies. Liv, if you want to get it out, it's in the cooler."

Liv made quick work of pouring Dorothy and herself a glass. "This is really good, Josh! What's in it?"

"Oh that's my secret recipe." Liv rolled her eyes and let the corner of her lips curl up in response. Josh tipped his head back in laughter. Liv brightened at the sound. It really did feel good to make him laugh. He allowed laughter to consume him, he nearly always laughed with his entire body.

"Well, whatever it is, it's quite good," Dorothy added, taking a prim sip.

"Oh hey! There's an eagle!" Josh turned on the automatic pilot and left the cockpit. He stepped toward Liv and leaned over her shoulder, resting his left hand on her upper back. Her skin softened to his touch instantly, as if she'd been frozen for years and he alone could bring back her softer, warm edges. Her instinct was to flinch, to pull away from a touch that was not Michael. After all, that's what a good wife does. That is what she had done for the tenure of her marriage. Willingly, and with pride. To override the feeling of being disloyal to Michael, to allow herself to let Josh touch her and to respond in kind, was harder than she imagined. But also felt right in the way that being alone for so long had begun to feel … wrong.

"Do you see it, Liv? The nest is just over here—at the top of that pine!" Josh leaned closer, urging Liv to turn her gaze farther, toward the trees. She could feel his breath on her cheek, as warm as the air. Goosebumps bloomed across her arms as she scanned the shoreline for the bird and his home.

"There he is! She? He?" Liv asked excitedly as she finally spotted the majestic bird.

"I don't know, I guess? I'm not up on my eagle anatomy." Josh laughed, and Dorothy and Liv did, too. There was something so easy and simple about laughing with others. Of finding a similar joy in the path of a giant creature. There were moments where life was just easy. It had been a long time since Liv had experienced this special bliss.

There it is again, thought Liv. That inkling, a pull on her imagination to bring her heart's stories to life. There had been so many challenges these past few years. Losing Michael, Bella, her writer's block, and now losing her home. Could it be that after all this time her writer's block was finally subsiding? Of course, that would be the ultimate irony. Her ability—no, not just her ability, her affinity to write returning just as it is too late to save her career and home and likely her relationship with Bella? Of course Liv knew it wasn't that simple. And she knew it didn't just return on its own. She also knew, somewhere in the flood of reasons why her imagination was coming back to life was the simple fact that she was finally stepping back into her own.

Liv watched the mighty eagle soar across the sky. The wind, which had picked up, didn't deter or determine her path—she flew where she wanted to go and she was headed there. On purpose. Liv took a deep breath and reached her hand up toward Josh. Feeling his warmth beneath her skin fortified her. She wrapped her fingers loosely between his. For this moment, she would just be. Be here, with Josh Hart, and a giant eagle. On purpose.

Liv tucked herself deep into the covers of her bed, pulling the blankets up around her chin and taking a deep breath. She closed her eyes, hoping to catch his scent, if just for a moment. For two years she'd done the same thing every single night as she crawled into bed to sleep. One last deep breath in hopes of bringing Michael to her, of keeping him alive and holding him close. Of course, she knew it didn't make sense. She'd washed the covers many times since the last night Michael lay here with her. And the simple course of the days, in and out, out and in for two years dulled the belief that it would work. Still, she tried.

She reached for the notebook tucked just under her mattress. It was the fourth one since she'd started writing their story and it was nearly full. Writing, what once had served as both work and pleasure now served

Summer Love

as an elixir to the pain of life without Michael. Somehow, with every word written, her world was beginning to open up. She should have known the answer to losing her words was to find them. She'd spent so much time looking, she had left no space for them to find her. Until now.

Today, on the boat, with Josh's hand threaded through her own, she had felt the last of their story—the Michael and Liv story—come to her. It would be a late night, but in the end, the sun would rise, and Liv would finally, finally be ready.

Chapter 28

No Michigan summer festival would be complete without a Journey cover band. *Don't Stop Believin'* rang out from the gigantic speakers lining the stage as the crowd sang along to every verse, fists held high in the air. This was Detroit's song, and everyone knew it.

Liv smiled as the pyrotechnics reflected off of her friend's faces. Lucy and Maggie had met her here at the amphitheater adjacent to the marina. She'd brought her picnic basket full of snacks—sliced cheese, jalapeño sausage, and cookies from The Local Cup—and Josh. She had brought Josh to the town concert and fireworks.

When she had finally put down full notebook number four and laid her head on her pillow to sleep, it had been nearly 5 am. She'd slept for a few hours and even though she should have been tired, she woke up easily. She'd run her favorite five-mile loop around town and made Bella breakfast—scrambled eggs and sausage—before she headed to her office to begin the task of

Summer Love

transferring her now finished manuscript into an electronic version. Although she wasn't sure what she would do with the finished product, she knew she wanted to have it in a more formal format—so she sat down and began transcribing and editing.

Somewhere along the way, she'd texted Josh. She hadn't thought about it really. She hadn't agonized over whether she should or she shouldn't. She hadn't worried what people would think or if Bella would be upset. More than anything she had realized, she wanted to spend time with Josh. It felt ... right? Natural? Who knew? She only knew that somewhere in the depths of transcribing and editing, she'd picked up her phone and invited Josh to the concert and fireworks with her and her friends that night.

Liv had to admit, the element of surprise had worked—at least for a moment. When Liv and Josh walked up to the duo at their meeting spot on the amphitheater lawn, Lucy had been rendered speechless and Maggie had simply smiled and giggled as she shook Josh's hand and then pulled him into a sideways hug. Her friends had welcomed him kindly, which she had expected.

"I am proud of you, Liv," Lucy cooed in her friend's ear as the band eased into a ballad.

"Proud of me? Why?" Liv's voice carried a teasing

hint.

Lucy tipped her head toward Josh as he chatted easily with Maggie, his long eyelashes fluttering in the light reflecting off of the stage. Maggie laughed at something Josh had said, and Lucy turned her attention back toward Liv.

"Not easy bringing him here, I'm sure." Liv gestured to the crowd. The crowd was full of their friends and neighbors. People who had known Liv her entire life, and Michael too.

"You know, I would have thought it would be difficult. I expected it to be. But, I don't know. Somehow it wasn't. I just did it."

"You, Liv Pennington, planner extraordinaire and keeper of all traditions and rules *just did it?*" Lucy laughed out loud, causing Maggie and Josh to turn and smile in question at the two friends.

"I know, right? I don't know. I was working this morning and I just—"

"Wait. You were working? I thought we weren't working? I mean … I thought your writing wasn't working. Or the words weren't working—" Lucy stumbled over her handful of words. "Help me out here, Liv," she demanded.

"I have been … writing." The manuscript was still freshly born in her mind, and Liv had been unsure what she wanted to do with it. Give it to Isla? Keep it to herself? Print it for Bella to have? Suddenly, with the lights of a very large and very eighties strobe light disco ball skittering across her friend's face, Liv knew.

"Actually, I think I need your help."

"My help?"

"Yep, let's talk later, okay?" Liv turned back to the music and started to sing along.

Chapter 29

"Your mom seemed really good yesterday. I know you are concerned about her memory—but I loved to listen to her old stories, the bootleggers and the Ford mistress." Liv wiggled her eyebrows up and down as she smiled at Josh. The concert was winding down, and the fireworks would start any moment. There was just enough time to adjust their seats from the view of the stage to a view of the big, open sky.

"She had a lot of fun. Thanks for spending so much time asking her questions, listening." Josh shifted his weight from one foot to the other. The smell of cotton candy mixed with the deep yeasty smell of elephant ears was quintessential July, and he smiled as she took a deep breath. If he closed his eyes it could almost be *that summer.* Josh, Liv, and a summer night stretching out before them.

"Oh my goodness, are you kidding me? She's delightful. And besides, the writer in me is always curious." Liv smiled.

Summer Love

"One thing I've learned over these past weeks with her is that it's so important to listen. She just wants to be heard. She wants to matter. You know, she made a life out of making her home the hub. The hub for me, my brother, and my dad. All of the sudden, she's living alone in her house, and the world really got ... small. I can't believe I didn't see it before—that I didn't come sooner."

"You know, when we are living our lives and the day in and day out seems monotonous and perhaps even a little boring, it still surprises us when it's over and everything has changed. When Bella left after Michael died, my house, my job, my life, all felt ... not just small, but insignificant. If I could just lose my husband, and my daughter could just move away, what was the point?" Liv reached up and touched Josh's arm.

"But there is always a point. Your mom, she's lived a really good life. I know she is so grateful you came. That you have spent this time with her. You know, as much as I missed Bella—and it was an unhealthy much." Liv laughed at herself as she patted her chest with her free hand. "I didn't want her to come home for me. I wanted her to be out there in the world, carving out a life for herself. Your mom wanted that too. So don't be too hard on yourself."

Josh smiled and pulled Liv in for a hug. "I did make

one decision. I'm moving her into an assisted living facility next week. It's time. Tara, she's from Dr. Cameron's office, came and did a safety assessment and helped us figure out what she really needs. And ironically, as I have been worrying over what to do, Mom had already contacted several places in the area on her own as well. So, we went out to her favorite earlier this week and she picked out her apartment. In the end, I came here to take care of her and she took care of herself for me."

"Us moms are like that." Liv smiled and gave his arm a gentle squeeze.

"Hey, Mom!" Bella grabbed her mom from behind, wrapping her in a hug. When Liv let go of his arm and turned her head toward her daughter, Josh felt the cool night air on his skin where Liv's hand had just been. It felt naked, empty and even though he knew it was too soon to feel that way, it just was.

"Well, hello, sweet pea!" Liv laughed. "Hi, Hannah." Liv greeted the handful of kids that had come up with Bella, introducing them each to Josh in turn.

"Bella, it's nice to see you." Josh smiled respectfully at Liv's daughter, holding out his hand to shake hers.

"Nice to see you, too," Bella answered. Josh thought he detected a tone of relief that he had not mentioned their first meeting.

Summer Love

"So what are you kids up to tonight?" Liv asked.

"Watching the fireworks, and then there is karaoke at the Lodge tonight which I think we're going to go to," Bella answered.

"Oh that sounds like fun!" Liv answered with perhaps a touch too much enthusiasm.

Bella reported she would be staying at Hannah's house tonight, and Liv just smiled and agreed. Josh resisted rubbing Liv's back in the moment. He hadn't wanted to upset Bella, but he also knew that Liv was worried and wanted to offer her some comfort. Hannah gave Liv a hug as Bella dished off a quick, "See ya later," to her mom, and as quickly as they came, they were gone.

"Was that Bella?" Lucy asked. She and Maggie had just finished a conversation with a mutual client —a bride and groom new to town who had also just bought a new house—and joined the conversation.

"Yep. Bella and Hannah and some kids I don't really know."

"Well, I'd say it's progress that she came and said *hello,*" Maggie added. "We are going to go a little closer to the water. Do you want to move the blankets?"

Josh watched as Liv smiled and followed her daughter as she walked down the hill and toward the front of the crowd. "She is always so eager to be in the thick of things." Liv turned her attention back to Maggie. "Yes, we will. The view is better for the fireworks down there. Why don't you two go down now, and I will pack up the picnic basket and we'll be down after that."

"You got it. We'll go save enough room for all four of us," Lucy added. "Don't take too long, I bet they start here shortly."

Liv bent down to the ground and began collecting the impromptu picnic the group had enjoyed.

"Bella seemed good," Josh said as he picked up a few stray napkins and plastic cups to deposit in the trash.

"She does. She's still kind of cool with me at times. Frannie will be back from Georgia on Sunday, and we have to go over the final punch list before listing with Lucy. So, I don't have much time left to tell Bella about the house. I'm pretty sure I won't be able to hide a For Sale sign in the front yard for very long, and that is coming sooner rather than later." Liv sighed.

"You okay down here?" Josh asked as he knelt down next to Liv and loosely wrapped his arm around Liv's shoulders.

Liv nodded her head. "I am. You know, just empty nest sadness creeping in, that's all." Liv smiled at him as she lifted herself up from her knees to stand. "And, to be honest, there is a part of me that's wondering what she's thinking and feeling right now. After she saw the two of us together."

Josh followed her up, his eyes full of understanding. "It has to be strange for her to see you standing here with someone else. I imagine it's more than strange, it probably comes with a whole lot of different emotions." Josh paused. "Even if we are just friends."

"Are we just friends?" Liv asked, her voice coy and timid at the same time.

"Didn't we have this conversation thirty years ago?" Josh laughed.

"Well, look how that turned out," Liv deadpanned back.

Suddenly, the sky opened up with brilliant packages of red, white, and blue fireworks. The embers exploded across the sky, banging and booming their flight into the night. The light sparkled up and over the inky black sky, reflecting nearly perfectly on the glass water. The thing about watching a fireworks show on the lake was that you got to see it twice—once in the air and once sparkling off the water's edge. Parallel shows, parallel lives. *Interesting*, he thought. Even though they were mirrored reflections of the same image–they weren't exactly the same.

Liv watched the sky, and Josh watched Liv, her eyes dancing with excitement as she tracked the bursts of color. Josh couldn't help but smile.

"Hey, Josh?" she asked.

"Yes, Liv?" Josh turned his shoulders toward Olivia. His arms tucked in together across his chest, and he smiled down at her.

"You never answered my question."

The grand finale burst into the night sky just as Liv finished her sentence. The sparks, brilliant and bold, painted the sky with strokes of color and light. Josh smiled and reached his hands out to touch Liv's cheeks. Cradling her face in his hands, he bent toward her. A lock of her hair fell into her eyes. He reached his thumb up and gently tucked it behind her ear, a smile playing on both corners of his lips.

Josh's heart raced—thumped, actually. It felt as loud inside his chest as the fireworks sounded in his ears. Both booming, powerful echoes of combustion. If he'd closed his eyes, he could have transported himself back in time, to his nineteen-year-old body, to a spot nearly exactly here, on this hill. To the night Josh first kissed Liv under the deep purple sky. There hadn't been fireworks that night, but there had been the deep, heady attraction that he felt again now, after all this time, seated deep in his core.

Liv tipped her head up toward his, an invitation that he took. His lips pressed so quietly on hers he wasn't sure he hadn't dreamt it. Still, their lips touched again.

Summer Love

This time without the trepidation of the first kiss in thirty years, but with the experience and knowledge of those same thirty years and all it had taught them.

Chapter 30

"You know I never told him about you," Liv blurted out. There, she'd confessed. For over thirty years she'd kept her secret to herself. Michael never knew about Josh. He never knew she'd fallen in love that summer. He never knew there had ever been anyone else. He never knew he wasn't the first.

Josh tipped his head sideways in question. The fireworks had finished, and the two of them had never made their way down to Lucy and Maggie. Liv hoped her friends wouldn't be upset—truthfully, she knew they would be rather excited. They had been waiting for her to move forward for a long time. And kissing Josh in the middle of the town fireworks certainly *felt* like moving on.

Liv paused to smell the carnival-scented air and started over. "I mean, I never told Michael about you. I never told him about that summer. Our summer."

"Okay …" Josh drew out the word as he squinted his eyes.

Summer Love

"I never told him because, well, it seemed like it didn't matter at the time. I was sixteen—well, seventeen when he came home. He had broken up with me to go to London. He hadn't wanted a girlfriend, he'd wanted to 'sow his wild oats' as my mother so bluntly put it in some strange effort to cajole me out of being sad about it when it happened. Of course, that's an entirely different story." Liv looked up into Josh's eyes and smirked. "I was certain he was over there having the time of his life."

"So our summer was because you were getting back at Michael?" Josh asked with just enough sarcasm to let Liv know he didn't quite understand what she was saying.

"I didn't choose a very good time to do this." Liv laughed as her hands fell to her side, and Josh let go of the cradle in which he had been holding her chin. "But I need to get this out."

"Again. Okay …" Josh's tone was laced with nervousness.

"I like you, Josh."

Josh smirked, "Are we in some weird time slip where we will keep having the same conversations we did that summer, just thirty years apart?"

"I know it sounds silly, but just listen. I haven't done this …" She motioned her hands between them and then looked into his eyes. "I haven't done this with anyone except Michael ... since you. And it's important for me to know that you know where I stand."

"Which is?" Josh asked quietly.

"When I lost Michael, when I found him on the floor, I ... I ... my world just fell apart. I threw myself into Bella and track and her scholarship—which turned out to not be the right thing to do—and I avoided anything that had to do with me. With my life. I felt—still feel—so guilty."

"Guilty for what? You surely don't feel guilty about our summer romance thirty years ago, do you?"

"Well, when you put it that way it sounds silly. Because, you're right. It was a silly romance—"

"I didn't say 'silly.' It wasn't silly. We were young, both of us. But I loved you, Liv. I did. I loved you as much as a nineteen-year-old kid can love."

Liv looked up into Josh's eyes, trying to read his thoughts. "I loved you, too." Liv took a deep heavy sigh. "I also loved Michael. And a part of me feels guilty that you always knew about him and he never knew about you. And a bigger part feels even guiltier that he never *knew*."

Josh nodded. While she hadn't said it, he understood what she was telling him. Michael never knew about the night Josh and Liv spent under the stars on

Harmony Beach.

"Liv, it's been nearly thirty years."

"Yes, and it's been two years since Michael died. And I've been stuck. And frankly, I think I would have happily *stayed* stuck if it weren't for you coming back to town. Something about seeing you again, of reminding me that life could be fun. That it didn't have to be all avoiding writing and grieving Michael. I just wanted you to know, I never told him about you and I always wondered why."

Liv watched as people milled around them like an island mid-river, as Josh waited for her to continue.

"Do you know why?" he finally asked.

"I do now." Liv took a deep breath as her hands shook, just a touch. Enough to remind her that she was alive and that this, jumping back into feelings and life, was frightening. But also wonderful. "I didn't tell him because you *mattered to me.* You were my first love. I'd been infatuated with Michael before that, but I hadn't loved him yet. I was too young. But my parents' divorce, that summer, I ... I grew up. And in so many ways, loving you paved a way for me to love Michael." Liv took a deep breath.

"I kept memories of you stashed away in the back of my mind. Hidden, just for me. Being married for so long isn't always easy—although Michael made it as easy as it could be. But there were days. Days I just wanted to be young and carefree. Days I just wanted to go back to working on the fuel dock and dreaming about what my life would be instead of knowing I'd already set my course. Maybe that's why I like to write so much. Because it gives me many lives to live." Liv laughed.

"The truth is, memories of you were an escape for me when things were tough. Remembering you reminded me of who I was before I was a wife and a mother. There were days I needed that. And Michael never knew that, but I need you to."

"I never forgot you, Liv," Josh said, echoing his promise from Harmony Beach all those years ago.

"And here you are. Again. Reminding me I am more than a wife—a widow—and a mother. Thank you for that."

"I don't think it's me you have to thank for that, Liv. I think you should thank yourself. You did this. You have gotten yourself through the last two years without your husband. You are figuring out a solution to your problems with the house, with Bella. You are." Josh traced her face with his finger, sending a feverish chill deep into Liv's belly. It had been a long time since she'd felt this way. "I would like to be a part of it, though."

"A part of—?" Liv asked.

"A part of the next chapter. A part of your story."

"You already are a part of my story, Josh."

"Do you remember why we broke up?" he asked.

Liv knitted her brows together. "I think we just came to the end of the road. Ours was a summer love, and we made it to September."

"You know, I love the fall," Josh said with a grin.

"You do?" Liv smiled and reached her arms up around Josh's neck. The stream of people had lessened to a very small trickle. The low din of the crowd's excitement faded into the parking lots and cars headed home. Liv and Josh were nearly alone.

"I do. I love a pumpkin spice latte—which I realize may be unpopular to some! I love apples and apple cider. I love hayrides and I love the changing leaves."

"Is that so?"

"And I'm sure I'd love to see the view of the lake in October."

"It's beautiful. The colors reflect so easily off the water. Do you know my favorite view of the lake?"

Josh shook his head, his eyes never leaving Liv's gaze.

"December. The winter. When the lake is blue with ice and covered in snow. You should see it sometime."

With that Josh laughed, leaned in, and kissed Liv.

Lightly at first, and then with every moment of distance between them and with thirty years of longing. And in that one kiss, their summer love picked up right where it left off.

Chapter 31

"How was Georgia, Frannie?" Maggie asked. Hannah was busy pouring four mimosas tableside for the Ladies of the Round Table. It'd been a few weeks since their schedules had coincided and all four women could meet.

"Georgia was good! Saw my momma and daddy, and they're doing well. Everything was fine." Frannie spun her champagne flute in a circle while her auburn hair was piled high in a messy top bun.

"So, how is Mamaw Dixie?" Lucy asked.

"She's amazin'. Ninety-six and still rulin' the roost. She loves her friends and all the activities at the home. I used to hate thinkin' of her there, but every time I go back and see her, I swear she looks better and better!"

"Aww, that's wonderful." Liv smiled.

"Frannie raised her hand to catch Hannah's attention. "Can we have another round?"

"Frannie. She just finished pouring this round. What's up with you?" Lucy questioned.

"I'm just a little frazzled is all. I'm trying to finish up the house for Liv so you can get it listed. I just have a lot on my mind." Frannie's voice teetered on testy, which never happened.

"Can we help at all?" Maggie asked, always the helper.

"No, y'all have enough on your plates. I'll figure it all out. It's fine."

"And we are back to fine." Lucy smiled her sarcastic twist of lip at Frannie and turned to add, "Hannah, you better go ahead and get us another round!"

"So what's up with you three? Anything exciting happen while I was gone?"

Maggie and Lucy looked at Liv and smiled.

"Liv? What's up? I've been at the house every day this week—you didn't say a word about anything exciting …"

"Liv? What did you do last night?" Lucy asked. Maggie smiled coyly.

"I went out to dinner."

"Where did you go out to dinner?" Lucy pressed.

"I went to Whiskey Harbor."

"Whiskey Harbor? As in the Whiskey Harbor Club that you can only get into if you are a member and it's super expensive?" Frannie laughed.

"Liv? Who did you go to Whiskey Harbor with?"

Frannie, Lucy, and Maggie all looked at Liv.

"I went ... I went with Josh."

"Josh? Circa 1988 Josh?" Frannie asked.

Liv laughed. "Yes, Josh circa 1988."

"Oh wait! On a date! You went on a date with Josh circa 1988?" Frannie exclaimed.

"Shhh ... You don't have to announce it to the whole world! My goodness. Yes, it was a date." Liv laughed, and her cheeks turned pink.

Hannah returned to the table with a second round of mimosas as the four women continued to pepper Liv with questions about her date and Josh circa 1988.

"What does Bella think of the newest developments?" Lucy asked.

"Well, I don't really know. I haven't gone out of my way to discuss it with her, and she hasn't asked any questions. She knows we do things together, of course. I just haven't gone into much detail. I don't know what *details* to give, and she isn't asking. So I have left it at that. Plus, I still have to tell her about the house—"

"Liv, you have to tell her about the house," Lucy said.

"I know. I know. And I know I should tell her more about Josh—I mean, she *knows* about Josh. She just doesn't *know* about Josh. I am walking on thin ice with her all the time, and lately she's been more pleasant than not, and I just don't want to rock the boat."

"Woah, that's a lot of analogies in one sentence." Frannie laughed.

"She knows something's going on. She's made a few comments to me about it at work. But I learned my lesson—I haven't said a thing and I'm staying out of it," Maggie added.

"I don't blame you, Maggie. Hey, how's Bruce the Jerk, by the way?" Lucy asked Maggie.

"You know, nothing much has changed. It just is what it is. I'm too tired to argue with him anymore. Frankly, I'm too tired to even talk about it." Maggie took a deep breath. "His mom did call and said she'd love to have the kids for spring break, so maybe I will do that next year. I don't know. I know she's trying to help and I know she feels terrible about what he did."

"Oh Mable. I love Mable," Liv answered. "I'm sure it kills her to see her son turn out to be such a …"

"Jerk?" Lucy finished with a scowl. Liv and Frannie nodded in agreement.

"He wasn't always a jerk," Maggie said with a quiet voice, her eyes trending down toward her naked ring finger.

"No, he wasn't, honey. He wasn't." Frannie wrapped an arm around her friend.

"I'm sorry, Maggie. I know he's the boys' dad. I

know he was your husband. And he wasn't always a jerk," Lucy conceded with a solemn nod.

"I just don't know how this ended up being my life. How did I end up being such a cliche? I am an overweight divorcée single mom who can't control her kids. I'm a hot mess."

Liv's heart squeezed at her friend's words. "Maggie, that's not how I see you—that's not how any of us see you!" Lucy and Frannie nodded in agreement.

"Does it matter? Does it matter if you don't see me that way if that's how I see myself?" Tears welled up in Maggie's gentle blue eyes.

"It does matter. It does," Lucy demanded.

"Maggie, after Michael died, I saw myself only as a widow. A widow and a mother. That's it. I honestly believed that if I did anything to change that, if I became a widow who dated or—heaven forbid—fell in love, I would be forgetting Michael. I would be diminishing what we had together. I was afraid if I started to really live my life again, people would forget Michael. They would assume I didn't love him the way I did, the way I still do and always will." Liv took a sip of her mimosa and wiped a tear from her eye with the side of her hand.

Lucy reached over and squeezed Liv's knee, and Frannie closed her eyes as she listened. "But Maggie, I was wrong. I wasn't serving Michael by not living my life. I wasn't honoring our marriage or even *his* life by sitting in my kitchen and trying to force words out of my hands. I didn't honor him by railroading my daughter into going to his alma mater and running on a scholarship she didn't want. And in part I did all that because of what I thought I was *supposed* to do. I definitely don't have it all figured out, but one thing I do know is that it doesn't matter one bit what anyone else thinks about me or Michael or Bella. Or even Josh. What matters is what *I* think. And it matters what you think. And you aren't thinking clearly."

"Maggie, Liv is right. I'm sorry I harp on Bruce. I'm just so mad at him for what he did to you. But the truth is, if this is who he really is—and it's clear that it is!—then we should be thanking him for getting out of the way." Lucy rubbed her friend's back as Maggie took a deep breath and used her napkin to wipe away her tears. "You are so much more than a cliché. You have to know that." Lucy looked at Maggie and then Liv.

"Y'all, listen. Maggie, bless your heart. You are one of the most amazing women I know. And I know at least three amazing women." Frannie smiled, and so did her friends. "And what matters is that when you see yourself in the mirror you need to see someone you are proud of. And you can't let a divorce or what you see as a little extra weight or two very rambunctious boys make you think you are less than you are."

"You're right. I know you're right. It's just really, really hard some days." Maggie nodded agreement to her own words.

And Liv added, "I couldn't agree more."

"How did you do it, Liv? How did you just keep going after Michael died? So many days I just don't want to even get out of bed and face another day alone. I liked being married. I liked being a wife. I loved having a family, all together."

"Oh Maggie. I have no idea. And I still struggle a lot of days to just keep going." Liv looked out the window and watched as cars drove by, bikers rang their bells through the main intersection, and window shoppers peeked in windows of stores that weren't quite open. "The world, it just keeps going no matter how sad or worried or anxious we are. It goes on even when the people we love are gone. But that's the gift, Maggie. That's the gift. You. *You* get to keep going."

Chapter 32

The forecast called for falling temperatures as a north wind blew in a storm during the morning hours. It wasn't unusual on the big lake to have north winds sweep down from Canada and deliver chilly, windy days. Let alone storms. Liv peeked out her kitchen window looking down toward the bluff. The sky was swirling with clouds, and the wind had shifted to gusts. Her American flag stood straight at attention. Yep, a north wind had arrived.

She would have to make her way to the beach to secure her Adirondack chairs and the umbrellas over the table and loungers before the wind had its way with them.

She pulled on a pair of leggings and a T-shirt and ran downstairs to grab a hooded sweatshirt. As she pulled it off the hook, she noticed Michael's favorite red buffalo pattern flannel that Liv had gifted to Bella a few weeks ago hanging on the last hook by the door. Smiling, she pulled it off the hook and brought it to her face, rubbing the soft fabric against her cheek. She slipped her tiny arms into each ample sleeve and pulled the edges close together in the middle.

She had come to peace with the fact that despite her efforts to live her life again, and despite how much she enjoyed and looked forward to spending time with Josh, the sadness that came with losing the love of her life would always be with her. The sadness came to her in different incarnations—sometimes bittersweet, sometimes exquisitely painful. Today it showered her in a soaking rain of gratitude that she had had him to love.

Climbing down the cement stairs that followed the bluff's rugged terrain toward the landing and the beach, she looked out across the vast lake. She would never tire of this view. Out deep in the water, she could see three freighters. As usual, her mind wandered back to Michael and the last sunset. She'd spent most of the past few weeks transcribing the four handwritten notebooks into an electronic document that she'd then asked Lucy to read. Lucy had always been a first reader for Liv because she held no punches. Her critiques were always well thought out and spot on. Being a voracious reader and a secret romantic at heart—as well as being one of Liv's dearest friends—made her the perfect candidate to be the first to read *The Last Sunset*.

Liv herself felt it was her best work, but also, it was a complete departure from her normal formula: woman meets man, woman falls for man, woman and man have a misunderstanding, woman and man make up and live happily ever after. She wasn't sure she was her own best critic when the story was her life. She'd given the manuscript to Lucy just yesterday, but still she was waiting on bated breath to hear what she thought.

Liv turned her attention to the task at hand as she worked feverishly to secure the chairs, wind down umbrellas, and haul them to the small shed that was nestled in the corner of their beach at the foot of the bluff. The waves were rolling in with force, some even rolling the twenty yards up the sand to where Liv worked, soaking her shoes and socks. This storm was brewing to be a big one. She knew Bella was at work but decided to text her daughter anyway.

Liv: Big storm rolling in. I've got everything buttoned down here. Be safe sweet pea

Liv tucked her phone away and finished hauling the lounge cushions and a few small items back to the shed before making her way back up to the house. At the top of the bluff she again looked out toward the lake. A giant shelf cloud was thrumming its way from the north across the water and right toward Blue Water Bay. The darkness that accompanied the storm had already begun to steal the early morning daylight as Liv hustled inside. Turning on a few lights, she hung Michael's flannel back up where she'd found it. The sleeves had gotten a little wet, and she wanted to be sure it was back where Bella had left it when she returned home. Throwing her phone on the kitchen counter, she realized she'd missed Bella texting back.

Bella: I'm at work. All good. Sorry you had to put everything away yourself.

Liv thought about the last part of Bella's message as she brewed a second pot of coffee. When Michael was alive, Liv never would have done storm preparation alone. He would have done it for or with her. Bella knew that, and it squeezed Liv's heart that her daughter recognized some of what Liv had taken on in the wake of her father's death.

Time was extremely short, and she had yet to tell Bella about selling the house, or about her budding romance with Josh. *Josh.* It *was* a budding romance! The last few weeks had been both exciting and confusing as Liv navigated life as a dating widow. For her part, Bella had been busy at work and with Hannah, so their paths had yet to cross at a point where Liv felt there was time and space to tell her daughter what she knew she didn't want to hear. Liv's stomach danced now at the thought of telling Bella everything. Things were peaceful for the moment, and Liv had no desire to give that up.

The wind picked up relentlessly outside. Liv gathered a few candles and filled a pitcher of water in case she lost electricity. Her phone buzzed again with a message.

Josh: Big one coming. You ok?

Liv: Yep! Just got everything buttoned down on the beach. Going to sit on the porch and watch it come.

Josh: Sounds perfect. Wish I was there.

Liv's belly flooded with warmth, and her hands began to sweat. She was no different now than when teenage Liv had dated Josh. A nervous, lovesick, giddy mess.

Out on the porch the rain began lightly. Just a few soft sprinkles covering the window panes. Liv tugged a blanket up onto her lap and pulled a book out from the drawer next to her chair. She thumbed through until she found the dog-eared page where she had left off and began to read.

Liv's attention waxed and waned through the next

few chapters as the storm pelted the porch and the bluff. Surging gusts of wind shook the house. While she wouldn't say she was scared, there was an element of foreboding. Nature was something wild, and that was never more present than on the lake's edge during a storm.

Liv put the book down and walked to the edge of the porch. The storm had been raging for nearly an hour, but finally the sky was beginning to lighten up and the rain was diminishing. Although, the wind continued to howl. She heard a crack, almost like lightning. Just as she turned to the south and looked out the window, it happened.

In the blink of an eye, the big oak was coming down. And it was headed straight for the house.

Chapter 33

The crack had been so loud that Liv was convinced that the big oak—the one Michael had taken Bella's picture next to on every first day of school—had come down completely. The power had flickered at the same time the tree was hit, making Liv nervous she would find her kitchen damaged—or even worse, demolished. She'd run back through the house from her porch into the kitchen, navigating her way carefully through the dim light, expecting to hear a gigantic crash along the way.

But she hadn't. Carefully she skirted through the house, making her way upstairs. She avoided where she thought the tree may be resting against the roof only to see out the bedroom window that the whole tree hadn't come down, but a branch the size of a fairly large tree had given way. Although some of the leafy branches had scraped the house on the way down, the main trunk of the branch was laying squarely across the driveway. Thankfully she had parked her car in the garage—otherwise, it would be under the branch. As it was, she wouldn't be moving her car until the tree was moved.

Liv climbed back down the stairs and found her phone in the kitchen. She'd no sooner picked it up than a text chimed in.

Josh: I think the storm has cleared. Lots of debris down over here. You okay?

Liv took a deep breath. Asking Josh for help at her house felt more akin to cheating on Michael than going to dinner with the man. She knew logically that made no sense, but still, she fidgeted for a moment before she answered.

Liv: Mostly okay.

Josh: What's wrong? I will be right over.

Liv: There is a huge branch down in my driveway. You may have to park on the street. Think tree-size branch. Not branch-size branch.

Josh: I'm on my way.

Three hours later, Josh and Liv were soaked with sweat and leftover rain from the leaves of the fallen branch. They had cut and hauled the entire branch themselves. They'd worked well together, Liv mused. And now she was exhausted. She looked up at Josh to see sweat dripping down his forehead. The cool breeze that had been left behind after the storm was already gone, and in its place was a sticky, humid, stagnant pool of air.

"That's good enough. At least I can get out of the driveway and Bella can get in when she gets home." She'd talked to Bella earlier and warned her of the mess in the driveway. Bella had been concerned at first, but Liv told her not to worry, she was getting help and would have it all cleaned up. Liv had stopped short of telling Bella her *help* was Josh, and Bella didn't ask.

"I can come back tomorrow and we can get the rest of this wood stacked up. You should have enough wood here for Bella to host the next year's worth of beach bonfires!" He laughed.

"Ha! Hey, I have an idea. Hold on." Liv ran inside and changed into a bathing suit and grabbed two towels and two large bottles of water. Thankfully, the power had returned sometime while they had been working in the driveway.

Handing Josh a bottle of water that he took gratefully and drank immediately, Liv asked, "How about a quick swim?"

"Sounds good to me. As thick as this air is, that may be the only thing that cools us down."

Liv smiled inside. She wasn't sure swimming with

Josh would cool her down at all.

The pair walked down the cement stairs, Liv surveying the damage to the foliage on the rugged edge of the bluff. Not much had been affected other than scattered small branches and leaves being blown down. Liv sighed a breath of relief. She needed the bluff trees and brush to be healthy to prevent erosion. Suddenly she remembered that soon the integrity of the bluff wouldn't be her problem anymore. A strange sense of doom and sadness settled on her as thick as the soupy air.

Liv's legs felt like they carried cement from the afternoon cutting, hauling, and stacking wood as she followed Josh down to the beach. She watched as he picked up random sticks, tossing them back into the wild edges over the stair rail. The sense of doom and sadness had bled into the soreness, and she was beginning to feel it in every muscle. It was a different sore than a long-run sore, and somehow it felt good. A productive, well-earned soreness. She was profoundly sad to lose her home, but stacking that sadness against losing Michael reminded her that she could handle what was coming.

Finally reaching the sand, the two hung their towels on the railing. There was some random debris, branches, and leaves strewn about the beach—but that would be there tomorrow. For today, they were done working.

Liv and Josh waded out into the water. The storm had rushed in a pile of stones covering up the typically sandy bottom under their feet. The sudden rocky terrain had Liv holding onto Josh's hand as she walked out to the sand bar. The water was cold, as expected, but also felt delicious.

"This is exactly what this old man needs." Josh said as he let go of her hand and let himself fade from standing to resting up to his shoulders under the water.

"Old man? Come on! You can't call yourself an old man because that would make me an old woman, and I'm *not* ready for that yet!" she teased.

"Okay. This is exactly what this tired man needs."

"Better." She smiled as she used her arms to push herself closer to him. She dove under for the last few feet. Under the water there was an organic stillness. As if nature was reminding her to take pause, to listen, to be quiet. She came up out of the water and floated on her back, using her hands to paddle herself against the gentle waves.

"It's crazy how rowdy the waves were this morning when I was down here getting ready for the storm. They were busting all the way up nearly to the bottom of the stairs. They have only reached up there a few

Summer Love

times that I can remember."

"It is especially crazy when you look at it now." Josh stood looking out toward the horizon. The water was still as glass with just a few quietly rolling waves coming in toward shore.

"All quiet until the next time," Liv said softly as they floated together silently for quite a while. Finally, the water having dispelled the heat of the afternoon and the soreness of the tree cutting, Liv spoke. "I am not much in the mood to cook but I can order us takeout for dinner—my treat to thank you for your help."

"You don't need to do that. The only thanks I need is seeing you in that bathing suit." Josh dove underwater and surfaced right next to Liv, circling his arms around her waist. Laughing, she wrapped her arms around his neck and rested her cheek against his. The pair gently bobbed in the water, feeling the tension of the storm and the work of the day literally floating away.

"Thank you for your help today. It was nice to not have to figure it out by myself," Liv whispered into his ear.

Josh pulled his cheek away and rocked his forehead on hers. He looked into her eyes with as much passion as Liv had seen in him when he was a young man, with the world ahead of him. Her stomach took flight with anticipation as his lips met hers. They stayed that way, encircled in each other, kissing, until the apricot sun began dissolving into the water.

Chapter 34

"I can't believe Nino's Pizza is still in business." Josh pulled a giant piece of New York style pizza apart from the rest of the pie. Cheese strung out in thick webs as steam rolled up into the evening air.

Liv and Josh were seated side-by-side on the picnic table near the edge of the bluff. Nothing remained of the epic storm. In fact, nothing but a gentle wind brushed through the trees, leaving them to faintly hear the roll of the waves down below.

"I know, right? It's so good!" Liv lifted her piece to her mouth, bending her head to take a bite.

"I can't remember being this hungry in a long, long time," Josh said as he took another sip of his beer in between bites.

The two ate in silence until nearly the entire pizza was gone. An entire afternoon of work and an evening of swimming and cooling off in the lake behind them, their dinner felt well earned.

"Do you think any of that wood would burn in a

fire?" Liv asked.

"Probably not, it's too green. But … I did see the remnants of a woodpile on the edge of the bluff when we were cleaning up. Mind if I start one using that?"

Liv smiled. "Michael stacked that wood there for Bella and her friends. He always wanted our house to be *the* house. You know? The house where all the kids hung out."

"He sounds like an amazing dad."

"He was. He was an amazing dad. An amazing husband. We—Bella and I—we were really blessed." Liv paused before going on. She supposed she should feel awkward at best talking to Josh about Michael, but she didn't. "Let's start that fire."

"You sure?" Josh asked, looping his arm around her shoulders and pulling her in toward his chest.

"I'm sure. No reason for that wood to go to waste. Leaving it stacked up there doesn't change the fact that Michael's gone. And burning it, well, it just feels right." Liv tipped her head toward Josh. Bella planned on coming home after work, but texted to let Liv know she had gone to the movies with Hannah and would spend the night there. Without Bella being home, Liv felt free to enjoy Josh's outward affection.

"You got it." Josh stood and began to build a fire inside the pit tucked in the corner of the property close to the bluff's edge.

"I have another idea," Liv called out. "I'll be right back!"

Once inside, Liv rummaged through the cupboards. Finally finding what she needed, she packed her picnic basket and headed back out toward the fire pit.

"I cleaned off these two chairs," Josh said, pointing to the ones looking out over the lake. "They were full of sticks and leaves and some walnuts from the storm. Okay to use them?"

"Great, of course! I have a surprise!" Liv lifted up the picnic basket in an offering. She opened the lid and first took out a bottle of red wine and two glasses. The flames from the fire flickered softly off the glass of each one. "I also have ... s'mores!"

Josh laughed as Liv set up an assembly of graham crackers, chocolate, and marshmallows on the small table sitting between the chairs. "I haven't had s'mores since my kids were little."

"They go perfectly with red wine." Liv handed Josh the bottle and the opener.

"And wine coolers, if my memory serves," Josh added.

Liv blushed. "Yes. And wine coolers. I'll go grab the marshmallow roasters and be right back."

Within a few minutes, Josh and Liv were nestled in

their respective chairs, roasting marshmallows and sipping a bold red wine. Liv had her feet tucked underneath her and a smile on her face. Despite all she had in front of her, she felt present. This moment was as perfect as moments get, inside the messy, sticky matter of life.

"So you *do* remember the last time we had s'mores?" Josh asked. His voice was low and sultry, just a hint of the memory playing at the edges of his words.

Liv closed her eyes and took another sip of wine. "Harmony Beach."

"Ummm hmmm …" Josh answered. The memory floated between the two of them, more feeling than words.

"We were so young then. So much life ahead of us. It's crazy to think of all that's happened. Me and Michael. You and Dina. Lacy, Zane, and Bella." Liv took a deep breath.

"What is it they say? The days are long but the years are short?" Josh asked.

"Gretchen Rubin," Liv answered.

Josh looked in her direction with a quizzical look as he gently pulled his marshmallow off of the poker and layered it with chocolate and graham cracker.

"Gretchen Rubin. The author. She said 'the days are long but the years are short.'"

"Well Gretchen Rubin is one smart lady." Josh took a bite out of his s'more, letting the cracker crumbs fall between his legs as he stretched the gooey marshmallow away from his mouth. "And also, whoever invented s'mores? Brilliant."

Liv followed his lead and constructed her own. The two ate in silence for a few minutes with only the crunch of graham crackers, the song of the crickets, and a few frogs in the distance.

"How's your mom?" Liv asked after they had cleaned their hands off and tucked away the s'mores makings into the picnic basket.

"She's good. She's settling into her new place. She joined their book club—she's actually requested they read one of your books." Josh smiled. "It's hard, you know, watching her age. My dad—I lost him quickly, and it was so soon after losing Justin I don't think I noticed him declining. It just felt like grief to me. I didn't see him *aging*. So, this is new to a certain extent. I'm not sure I like it. Well—I don't like it. But I think I don't like it in some respects for a selfish reason."

"I have a hard time finding you selfish," Liv whispered.

Josh turned and caught her gaze across the dancing fire flames. "Hmm ... well, I am. Sometimes."

"Tell me about why you think you are selfish."

"It moves me to the next rung. When I lost my grandpa—my mom's dad—I had that same feeling. I felt a buffer, I suppose, when I still had a head of the family a few generations above me. Now, with my mom, I'm starting to realize how far *I've* moved up the ladder. My children will have children before I know it. Time, it just stretches out forever and draws thin in the same moment."

"What will you do with the house?"

"Nothing for now." Josh took the last sip of his wine and put his glass down on the table between them. "I can continue to work remotely for now. I will have to travel some, but I'm just going to wait. Wait and see what happens before I do anything … permanent."

Liv took a deep breath. This was as close to discussing a future as they had come, and she knew from the look in his eye and the energy that surged between them that his waiting was about *her*. The thought both thrilled and terrified her.

Josh reached across the small table and took her hand in his, running his thumb across the back of her fingers in a gentle motion meant to comfort. Somehow, the comfort turned into heat, and Liv found herself aching for his touch beyond her hand. But she wasn't ready yet. She knew she wasn't and she knew she didn't want to ruin what they were building—with new and old bricks—because she was impatient. She could wait. She needed to wait.

"I'm so glad that tree didn't fall on my house," she proclaimed.

Josh laughed out loud. "Yes, that would have been bad. When is Lucy planning on listing again?"

"Soon. Frannie is coming over tomorrow to finish the punch list we agreed on a few weeks ago. Most of it is done. We were waiting on some parts and such. So, just a few more odds and ends to finish, and then Lucy will take the pictures and get it listed. I'd like to get it up before the end of the summer party—but that may be pushing it."

"I forgot about that … the Labor Day End of Summer Kickoff Party, right? Is it still down at the marina?"

"Oh yes, big deal, you know. We love our town gatherings here in Blue Water Bay." Liv tipped her head back as she laughed. Her body was warm and soft. Between the day's work and the wine, she was as relaxed as she'd been in months.

"I love it. I think it's …" Josh paused for effect. "Charming."

"It *is* charming! I love living in a small little town."

"I think I would, too." Josh's words were simple. But packed with meaning. He leaned over and kissed Liv on the forehead. She closed her eyes in pure bliss.

He tipped her chin up toward him and kissed her again. The comfort of a tired body, the warmth of a glass of wine, and the sweet taste of a summertime s'more on his lips was the perfect ending to a night filled with promise.

Liv stood and gathered her blanket and the two wine glasses while Josh collected her picnic basket and the marshmallow roasters. He swung his arm around her shoulders and kissed her on the top of her head. "I'm so glad I came back to Blue Water Bay."

"Me, too …" Liv smiled as she rolled her tired head into his chest.

"Let's get you inside. The fire is just about out, and you are exhausted. You've got a lot to do before this house goes on the market."

"What do you mean 'before this house goes on the market'?"

The words startled both of them—coming out of the dark. As Liv's eyes adjusted from the glow of the fire to the darkness in front of her, she realized that Bella was standing behind them.

And she'd heard every word.

Chapter 35

"Bella! What are you doing here? I thought you were staying at Hannah's?" Liv's words tumbled out like the contents of an overfull purse.

"Obviously." Bella's tone was sarcastic and caustic. Her eyes darted between Josh and Liv, the glow from the dying fire just enough to show her anger. She crossed her arms in front of her as she spoke.

Liv took a step away from Josh, widening the gap between them as he let his arm fall from its protective place across her shoulders.

"Let me just take this stuff inside and I'll get going," Josh said, his voice calm and clear. He looked toward Liv, their gaze catching long enough for Bella to see.

"No problem, *Josh*. I'll take care of it." Bella reached across the space between them and took the picnic basket out of his hands.

"Bella. Don't be rude," Liv said.

Bella laughed as she stood waiting for Josh to make his exit, her dark eyes steeled on her mom. It was clear she would not give them the luxury of a private goodbye.

"I'll call you tomorrow, Liv. Thanks for dinner." He rubbed his hand on her back, gently squeezing her shoulder before he took leave. "Goodbye, Bella. It was nice to see you."

Liv felt an enormous flush of gratitude for Josh. He hadn't taken the bait of her daughter's over-the-top reaction—instead he'd been calm and kind.

"Bye, Josh," Bella quipped over her shoulder quickly before turning her fury over to her mother.

"Care to explain, Mom?" Bella dropped the picnic basket on the ground then walked over to the fire pit, and threw herself in a chair.

"First of all, Bella, I am a grown woman and I am your mother. And no matter how upset you are at me—"

"Save me the lesson in manners, okay? Just tell me what he was talking about. What was he talking about, Mom?" Her voice lilted up in frustration as tears crept into her eyes. The tough teenager act of a few moments ago dissolved as quickly as the fire had to embers, and Bella sat with her arms crossed, staring into the glowing gray ash.

"Bella … I … I …"

"Just tell me."

"I have to sell the house."

And with that, Bella's shoulders caved with enormous heaving sobs. Liv felt her own heart rip to shreds as she watched her daughter realize the home she'd always known would be gone.

"Why? Why do you have to sell the house? Does this have to do with him? Does this have to do with Josh?" Her voice rose with panic. "Are you moving in with him or something?"

"No. Not at all. It has to do with me." Liv took a deep breath. She had long since promised herself she would never tell Bella about the loan her father took out on the house before he died. She had wanted to protect Michael. She had wanted to keep his memory pristine in their daughter's eyes. But in this moment, with the pain pouring out of Bella's heart into her own, she made a decision. Michael did not need protecting. And Michael wasn't perfect. He would never have wanted her to sacrifice her own relationship with Bella to save some Norman Rockwell version of himself. Like a coming sunrise, it dawned on Liv exactly what she had to do.

"It has to do with me, and your dad."

Over the next few hours, and deep into the night, Liv and Bella sat around the fire—Liv having stoked it after adding more logs from the stack of wood Michael had left. Liv told Bella about the loan Michael had taken, her advance and contract, her writer's block and the result: that the house must be sold.

Bella sat silently for a large part of the conversation, her anger dissolving into quiet, resolute sadness. Liv had spent all summer fearing Bella's anger and resentment. She'd hidden the truth to protect her daughter for as long as she could, only now did she realize that the truth was the only thing that could set them free of the constant teeter-totter they had been on. She should have known better.

"This isn't just yours and dad's fault. It's mine, too."

"Bella, no part of this is your fault. We are adults. We made the best decisions we could at the time, and they didn't turn out the way that we thought they would. This is not your fault."

"I should have spoken up. I should have told you I didn't want to run, that I didn't want to go to U of M. That would have saved a lot of money."

"Well, yes, that would have. But we both know I didn't give you any space to say your piece, and I can't expect you to have spoken up against your dad's alma mater and a running scholarship without my support. I'm just sorry I went full steam ahead with his dream and never asked you … about yours."

"Do you see the freighters? I can see the lights way out toward Canada," Bella asked, her voice small and child-like. If Liv closed her eyes, she would have sworn they had slipped into the past, somewhere in another lifetime where Bella was still a small girl.

Liv turned her head upward, twisting back and forth to catch sight of the line of red lights that outlined the ship. "Oh yes, now I do. Right over there, right?" Liv pointed toward the south.

"I never really liked them until Dad died. I know that sounds weird but I never thought they were anything special. But now, I think of him every time I see one, and that makes them super special."

"I agree."

Mother and daughter sat quietly together, the cool night air still and settling. The fire crackled just a whisper as its flames dwindled again to coals.

"I miss him."

"I miss him, too," Liv answered.

Waves of Bella's sadness washed over Liv as easily as the waves did while she floated in the lake today—which now felt like a lifetime ago. A ping of guilt shot through her when she thought about floating there with Josh while she watched her daughter physically grieve in front of her. While losing the house was no comparison to losing Michael, the grief was no less real. Liv hated that Bella would have to handle such loss twice in as many years.

"I'm afraid when we have to leave this house it will be harder to remember him."

"I understand. I won't ever let that happen, Bella."

"How can you be sure of that? If we move out of here and you … you move on with Josh, how can you promise he won't be forgotten?"

Liv had found answers to all of Bella's questions tonight, and somehow every time she'd asked, she'd known what to say. It was as if Michael had scripted the words in her heart, helped her write the play. Until now. Liv took a deep breath, searching for what to say. Searching for the right words to be the balm that soothed her daughter's soul. She looked deep into the fire, the flames again dwindling to a slow burn amongst the ashes. Her eyes grew tired with the work and heat of the day and the emotion and drama of the night.

She searched her body for a corner where she had hidden the peace from earlier in the day. She looked for a pocket that she could curl up in inside her own soul that would comfort her the way Josh and the waves and the cool water had earlier today. But she couldn't find that place. Instead, she found the truth. A truth she didn't want to hear.

It didn't matter that she finally found herself ready to move on with Josh; it only mattered that Bella was not. And Liv had to put Bella first.

Chapter 36

For three days straight, Josh called Liv. She never answered, opting instead to text back.

Liv: Sorry! Just jumping in the shower, I'll call you back.

Liv: Bella just walked in from work—can I call you back?

Liv: I'm working, I'll call you back.

By the fourth day after Bella had found them by the fire, Josh's morning call didn't come. Liv found herself oddly numb to the reality of it all. She could see the Liv who was ready. The woman who kissed Josh in the lake and sat easily next to him by the fire, eating s'mores. The woman who ached for him to touch her and the one who had vowed to give their romance time to bloom and not rush it. The woman who had suddenly found herself ready to move forward with Josh. She could see her in the mirror when she looked back at her reflection. That woman knew being with Josh was right.

But it, of course, couldn't be right. Not when it caused Bella such obvious pain. She knew she was being a coward by not confronting the issue and calling Josh herself. In fact, she knew she was worse than a coward, she was being hurtful. Hurtful to the boy who had loved her and the man who had given her a second chance to love again. Liv wasn't sure when her inherent courage had abandoned her. What she did know was that she had made a decision and it was time she owned up to it.

When Josh answered the phone on the second ring of the fifth day after the storm, Liv found herself speechless. His voice, the low and solid timbre, sparked a heat so deep in her chest, she thought if she hadn't lost Michael she might believe this to be the deepest ache a broken heart could give.

"Hi, Josh," she said, her voice laced with emotion.

"Hi, Liv," he answered.

"You know, Josh—"

"Liv—don't. You don't have to explain. I understand."

"You do?" she asked, her voice now echoing the ache she physically felt. Her palms were sweaty, her phone slipping in her grip. How could she let him go when she wanted so badly to pull him close? *Bella*, she thought. She would do anything for Bella. She hadn't done right by her daughter in the aftermath of Michael's death. She would do right by her now.

"I wish you well, Liv. I do. I treasured our first summer together for thirty years. And I will treasure this one, too."

"I just—"

"Liv … it's okay." And with that, the boy she loved and the man she'd fallen for hung up the phone for the last time.

Chapter 37

"Everything looks great, Frannie!" Lucy exclaimed. Lucy, Liv, and Frannie were touring Liv's house, surveying the work Frannie had been doing over the summer. The kitchen sink no longer dripped (that one took three tries to fix!); the cupboards all had handles and their tracks were straight. A few bedrooms had been painted, and the railing on the back porch had been bolstered. The house was ready to sell.

Liv looked out the window at the yard service mowing the lawn and weeding her sorely neglected flower beds. There were three workers; two were old employees of Michael's. She watched as the third, a young man in Bella's class, trimmed his way around the stone fire pit in the yard. He dragged each of the chairs away as his partner mowed the grass around it.

It had been two weeks since Liv and Josh's last conversation. She had seen him twice about town. Once as he sat in his car at the intersection before he turned toward the marina, and once walking out of The Local

Cup. It had been seeing him walk out of The Local Cup that had thrown her for a loop. He had been holding the door open for Angela. They both wore carefree smiles on their faces and were chatting, sipping their to-go coffees. She watched as they walked down the street together. All the while a deep pang of feeling sliced through Liv. Surely Josh wasn't *interested* in Angela now that they were over. He couldn't be.

But then again, Liv considered. Angela was free. She'd never been married, never had children. She was ten years younger than Liv and there was no ignoring the fact that her long legs and blonde hair made for a stunning package. Maybe he was. In the end, it wasn't Liv's concern anymore. She sighed heavily as she continued to watch out the window.

"Liv? Earth to Olivia?" Lucy was waving her hands in front of Liv's face.

"Oh, I'm sorry. I got distracted." Liv took a deep breath and pasted on a smile. "What were you saying?"

"I was saying that Frannie did a great job getting the place ready to sell. There is nothing left on our punch list as far as repairs go. I still need you to do a little decluttering and maybe take down a few of the family pictures. I have the paperwork for you to sign over here on the counter. I'll plan on putting the sign in the ground sometime in the next few days."

"Sounds good, Luce. Thank you. And yes, I agree, Frannie did a great job." Liv did her best to join the conversation. It was, after all, about her home, and these were her best friends trying to help her. But concentrating felt like walking through a sticky spider web. Her focus couldn't find purchase.

"I set up a few showings this next week for you, Liv. There are two really hot properties I want to get you into as soon as possible," Lucy added.

"Oh?"

"A condo up in Franklin and one in my complex that is a pocket listing here in town. That one in particular will probably sell the day it goes up—so to have the opportunity to see it before it even goes to market is a big deal. You will need to be ready to move on that one if you want it."

"But I can't buy anything until this sells," Liv added.

"Liv, this house is going to go fast. Very fast. You need to be prepared to make quick decisions."

"I don't know about looking in Franklin? It's a ways away from town, and Bella is planning to continue working at Beyond Blooms for the time being—and I don't know. Something about moving out of Blue Water Bay just feels … wrong."

"I know, I just want you to look. Okay? You get a lot

more for your money up there, and frankly, Bella isn't going to live with you forever and you can write anywhere. It's not so far that we won't see each other the same. It could be a fresh start. Will you just look at it?"

"I do quite a bit of work up in Franklin. The drive isn't bad at all," Frannie added with a small smile.

Liv looked from Lucy to Frannie, her throat tight with emotion. Frannie closed the small gap between them and wrapped her friend in a hug.

"Listen, I know it's hard. But Maggie, Lucy, and I are all here for you. We're going to the showings with you and we'll help you choose. You can do this. It will be excitin'! A fresh start. Who doesn't love a fresh start?" Frannie shook Liv's shoulders to make her smile.

Liv's lips turned up on the corners for a moment. "It is hard. It's really hard. And Bella is just so quiet. It's like a library in this house. I hate it."

"Have you spoken to Josh?" Lucy asked quietly.

"No. I haven't. Not since I told him I couldn't see him anymore."

"Are you sure that's what you want to do? You were coming alive again, Liv. Even though you lost your book contract and the house … even through all of that, that special Olivia Pennington sparkle was coming back." Lucy asked.

"Bella isn't ready. It's too much to ask her to swallow losing her house so soon after losing her dad *and* accepting that I am—was—dating again. I just can't do it to her. I wasn't always the most natural mother." Liv looked up at both of her friends, who both wore looks of disbelief. "I really wasn't, you know that's true. But I love my daughter with all I have and I have to make things right between us before I can introduce anyone else into my life. It just has to be that way." Olivia took the ends of her long bangs and tucked them behind her ears.

"What if she's never ready?" Lucy asked. "What if she never *wants* you to move on?"

"Well, then ..." Liv paused. "I'll deal with that if and when it happens. I have to give her a chance to adjust to it. I honestly don't think she ever considered it a possibility."

Frannie, Liv, and Lucy took one more last walk around the outside of the house, noting a few things that needed to be addressed in the next few days by the yard crew. Frannie said goodbye to Liv and Lucy before heading off to her next job site.

"You know, Liv, I didn't say anything when Frannie was here, but there is something I want to talk to you about."

Liv crossed her arms in front of her, tucking each

hand in close to her body. "Okay, what is it?"

"I finished your manuscript."

"You did?" Liv's heart began to race. She'd waited and waited to hear back from Lucy about *The Last Sunrise,* but between the punch list, the yard guys, and talking about Bella and Josh—Liv had momentarily forgotten about her next project. "What did you think?"

Lucy reached her hand out to take ahold of Liv's. "Let's go back inside to talk."

Liv nodded in agreement and took Lucy's hand in her own.

"I loved it," Lucy said.

"You loved it?" Liv asked, her voice breathless.

"I loved it. Whatever writer's block you had? It's gone. This is the best thing you have ever written." Lucy took Liv's hand in hers. "Liv, it's beautiful and heartbreaking. It's you at your best. You have to give it to Isla."

"Oh, I don't know about that ..." Liv wrung her petite hands together; they spun in and out of each other quickly. "It's so personal. It's so ... raw. I don't know if I can share that. It would feel like I was standing in front of everybody ... naked."

Lucy giggled. "I think I understand. I do. But I think you should at the very least think about it."

"Selling it seems, I don't know, wrong? Like I'm trying to profit from Michael's death, I guess? I don't know."

"I suppose you could go through it and remove some of the most intimate or vulnerable parts. But I'm telling you, Liv, it's beautiful. And I can see it helping other women. It will help Bella."

Liv's brow pulled together in a question. "What do you mean?"

"Liv, you have a way with words that most people don't. And yes, your romance novels are fun and spicy and they bring a lot of pleasure to people. But Liv, this is a life-changing piece of work. So many women lose their husbands. But not all of them can put into words the way that changes who you are the way you can. You'd be giving words to women who don't have them. Right when you thought you didn't have any more to give—you've come up with your most valuable words yet. And Bella? Bella will get to see—in a way most kids never do—the love you and Michael had for each other. It will help heal her, too."

Liv turned the idea over and over in her mind. She'd

have to read the manuscript again. She'd have to really be sure she was ready to bare her soul to the world, to Bella. Still, she couldn't help but feel the small spark of … excitement? Fire? Hope? Maybe sharing her story was what she was supposed to do.

"You think so?" Liv asked.

"I know so," Lucy answered. "So what do you say? Are you going to call Isla?"

Liv looked down at her hands. She squeezed them into a fist and then stretched them out again. Reaching up, she tucked a lock of hair behind her ear and stretched her neck back, looking up at the ceiling. Could she? Could she send this to Isla? Could she let the world—including Bella—read their love story?

"I don't know, Luce. I just don't know."

Chapter 38

Liv busied herself by stacking up a pile of photographs she'd taken off of the corkboard that had been stationed by the back door. She'd taken care not to go down the rabbit hole of looking at each one. Instead she pulled them off and turned them upside down. She'd tuck them away and bring them out some afternoon once they were settled in their new house. "I think this is the last box, Mom," Bella said as she plunked a cardboard box down on the kitchen counter.

"Oh thanks, sweet pea. At least by decluttering now, we won't have to do so much packing up when we move."

"Oh goodie," Bella answered, her lips turned down on each side as they had been for weeks.

Liv and Bella had spent the better part of their afternoon decluttering and depersonalizing the house like Lucy asked. Maggie and the boys had stopped by earlier to bring lunch, and Lucy had breezed in just after that to check in. Frannie had called on her drive into Franklin for a job. Liv smiled at the love she was feeling from her friends. Selling the house sucked. It really did. But somehow she felt like it was all going to be okay. Looking back at her daughter, Liv wished she could convince Bella of the same thing.

The work had been monotonous, sorting through items, packing some, throwing away others, and piling the rest up for charity. Liv had let her mind wander very little. She'd stayed focused and homed in on the present—it was a skill that had become more important since Michael died, literally equating to her survival somedays.

Except for the moments where she replayed her conversation with Lucy yesterday about her manuscript. Lucy had sent her a text message late last night, again encouraging her to send the draft to Isla. There were moments when Liv felt that familiar excitement she'd always had when a new project left her nest and flew to the next stage—when she knew it would eventually make it to her reader's hands.

But this book was different. It was personal. And she knew she had to be truly ready to share it, and to let it go if she called Isla. She couldn't breach her contract *and* send her a manuscript she didn't intend to publish all in a few months. She knew she had to be sure, and she wasn't yet.

"Are you hungry for some lunch? I guess it's kind of

late, maybe we should call this dinner? I can make you your favorite grilled cheese and my famous tomato and sweet corn soup? I have some saved in the freezer. It won't take me but a few minutes."

"I guess," Bella answered.

Liv pulled out a loaf of Italian bread she'd picked up at the farmer's market. It was just on the edge of stale—the best kind to make grilled cheese. She buttered each side and layered Havarti, smoked gouda, and cheddar before placing it on the griddle. The soup was beginning to thaw, and Liv stirred it carefully on the stove.

Bella continued to sit quietly as her mom made dinner. She fiddled with her phone and even asked if Liv wanted some help. Liv observed her daughter with a watchful eye. Today, working together had been far more pleasant than Liv had anticipated. Liv had been careful to tread lightly on any topics of importance. It was enough to be taking down family photos and packing up the extra shoes, coats, and sweatshirts hanging in their mudroom.

For Bella's part, she'd done what Liv asked her willingly. While she was not necessarily pleasant about it, she hadn't been disagreeable. Liv could see her daughter's attitude changing, and she was afraid to push too much. So, she'd weathered the occasional snark from her teenager and tried her best to be patient. Now, sitting around the kitchen island for a meal that Liv recognized may be one of their last in this home, she felt compelled to say what had been in her heart all day.

"You know I'm sorry, Bella. I never meant for any of this to happen."

Bella looked up from her phone slowly. As if Liv's words were hard to register. "Well, obviously you didn't mean for any of this to happen, Mom. I'm not blaming you … it's just …" Bella's words trailed off in a teenage haze.

"It's just that you do blame me," Liv said, stepping away from the stove and slinking down in the chair next to Bella at the island. "It's okay. I blame myself." Liv took her hand and twisted her watch around her wrist before she pulled her fingers through her hair. The weight of the last two years showed up when she least expected it. Like when she was making grilled cheese and tomato soup.

Bella slid back in her chair, her forehead resting on her crossed arms. "I know I'm being a brat."

Liv laughed and stood up, walking back toward the stove to stir the soup and flip the sandwiches. The sizzle from the griddle was familiar, and the smell of melted cheese and butter toasted bread mixed with the soup made Liv's stomach growl. "We are quite a pair, aren't we?"

Bella smiled. "Mom, I don't want you to blame yourself. And I don't want to blame you either. You aren't even the one who took the loan out on the house. Dad did."

"Yes, he did. But he did it with the best intent—and a plan! I am the one who spent the savings we had to force you to go to U of M. And I'm also the one who didn't sit down and write a book when I needed to."

"Yeah, well I'm the one who failed out of college." Bella rocked her head back and forth on the granite countertop. "That sounds gross when I say it out loud. Dad would be so disappointed."

"I don't know, sweet pea. I mean, of course he would be disappointed that you failed out. He never liked to see you fail at anything you tried. But he also knew failure is just a part of the game. And frankly, I don't think you would have even *gone* to U of M if he had been here. He would have listened. You would have spoken up. He was just better at ... that," Liv added.

"Maybe." Bella's voice was tinged with tears. "I do miss him. I miss him every day. But also ... I'm mad."

"I know you're mad at me, sweet pea. I know you are—"

"No, Mom. You don't understand." Bella lifted her

head up and looked at her mom. "I'm so mad at Dad. He just left us. He just left."

Liv sat stunned, looking toward her daughter. The silence of the room felt both insular and frightening.

"He just left, and I know he didn't want to, but it still happened and I am so mad at him for that. And I know it's weird and wrong and maybe even a little bit crazy but … it's the truth. And I've been taking it out on you all summer and I'm sorry, I'm just really sorry." Bella stood up from where she was and walked over to her mom.

"Can you forgive me? Please?"

"Forgive you? Forgive you for what? Having feelings? Being confused about how you felt when your dad died? I will not forgive you because you don't need to be forgiven for that. But I will love you. Every day. And all the days after that."

Liv wrapped her arms around her daughter and hugged her with all of the love she'd felt from that first day she'd been laid on her chest. Liv had never wanted to be a mom, but in the end, it was all that mattered to her. You didn't always get what you thought you wanted in life, but as it turns out, what you get is what you need.

"But, I will forgive you for your bad attitude at times." Liv smiled, and Bella laughed.

"I guess I deserve that."

"You do. Come on, let's finish this up so we can get up to the festival."

"Yes, ma'am."

Chapter 39

The Labor Day End of the Summer Kickoff Party wasn't nearly as exciting as the *beginning of* Summer Kickoff Party. Although, there was a certain comfort as you end summer and turn the corner toward fall. Autumn in Michigan is striking, and the colors on the leaves, the cooler temperatures, and football games were just as much fun and as beautiful as a good day in July. Still, the melancholy of the end of summer was as thick as the smell of elephant ears and cotton candy at the fair that lined the main street and stretched down to the marina.

Liv and Bella had come downtown together—they'd finished all of their decluttering and packing and were satisfied with the way the house looked to show. Lucy already had a showing scheduled for the following Tuesday morning, which was both exciting and nerve-wracking.

"Do you want to go grab something to eat? Are you hungry?" Liv asked Bella.

"Umm let's wait for Lucy and Frannie and Maggie. Are the boys coming?"

"Yes, I think so."

"Sweet!" Bella answered.

Liv and Bella walked up the street, saying hello to neighbors and friends. Hannah joined them for a short while before heading over to The Local Cup to help out. With the strong showing at the party, The Cup would be busy. Bella promised to catch up with her later, and Liv was grateful that her daughter was spending some time with her BFF again. The shorter days of fall were coming, the sunlight was dimming into the evening, and the cool air blew gently, reminding folks that the dog days of summer were coming to an end. September was nearly here.

Fall. Josh had told Liv how much he loved the fall. Liv couldn't help but feel wistful as she walked the streets of Blue Water Bay. Her eyes scanned the crowd looking for Josh, her heartbeat thumping deep in her chest at the opportunity to see him while her mind dreaded the idea.

Suddenly, next to Liv, Bella was nearly tackled from behind by not one, but two ten-year-old boys.

"I guess they are here!" She laughed. "Hey! No fair! Two against one!" Bella turned around and hugged both of the boys as they squirmed and laughed. "Do you guys want to ride any of the rides?"

"Mom said we have to have somebody ride with us and she won't do it," Carson said, his lips in full pout.

Cash clasped his hands behind his back and twisted his body back and forth. "But you could take us, Bella!" He smiled from ear to ear as he sang each word of his request.

"Do you want me to take them on some rides, Maggie?" Bella asked as the twins' exhausted mom walked up to join the small group.

"I would love for you to do that, but you need to understand you may be taking your life in your own hands." Maggie wiped her hand across her forehead where a sheen of sweat had already collected. Her blond hair bounced with each step she made.

"We will be fine!" Bella laughed. "Come on guys, let's go get some tickets and decide what we want to ride."

Maggie handed Bella some cash, and they made plans to meet back up by the popcorn stand in an hour.

"They are going to be the death of me. They bounced off the walls all day today. And while I'm so grateful Bella took them on rides, I will now spend the next sixty minutes worrying they will catapult themselves from the top of the Ferris wheel. I have no balance in my life. None. I'm either exhausted when they are around or missing them and worried for their safety when they are gone." Maggie reached over and hugged Liv. "How are you doing? Did you finish all of the packing up that you needed to do?"

"Yes, we did. We actually had fun. No, strike that. We didn't have *fun,* we had ... well, it just felt good to work together. To be on the same team," Liv answered.

"That sounds better than fun to me." Maggie smiled.

"Hello, Ladies of the Round Table! How y'all doin'?" Frannie sauntered up to the pair with a bag of pink and blue cotton candy. "Want some?"

"No thanks, that stuff is so sweet it makes my stomach hurt." Liv laughed.

"I'll take a little," Maggie answered, diving her hand into the bag of wispy sugar.

"Any of y'all know where Lucy is?" Frannie scanned the crowd looking for the last of their group.

"She's over there, I see her." Maggie pointed down the middle of the street. Lucy was still in work clothes and had her purse slung over her shoulder.

"Well lookie here." Lucy laughed. "It's the four of us. Just like old times. Please excuse my attire, my last client ended up putting in an offer and it took longer than expected, and I didn't want to take the time to go home and change."

"Nobody's worried about what you're wearin', Luce," Frannie drawled, offering her the bag of cotton candy."

Lucy reached in and took a small pinch. "Are we ready to take on the games?"

"We were born ready," Frannie quipped.

For the next hour the four women walked around the fair, chatting with neighbors and friends. They tried the ring toss—Maggie missed them all, Lucy got two of four, Liv got one, and Frannie got all four, earning herself a white teddy bear with a pink T-shirt that said "I love Blue Water Bay".

"Anybody want an elephant ear?" Liv asked.

"You can't eat cotton candy but you'll eat fried dough with sugar dumped on it?" Frannie chided Liv.

Liv laughed. "Yes. Yes I will. It's a special occasion! End of the summer and all that. Anybody else?"

With no takers, Liv arranged to meet them at the popcorn stand at the same time Bella would be back with the boys. Winding her way through the street, Liv waved to a few neighbors, nodded her head and politely smiled at Angela, who was chatting voraciously with Duncan Waldron, the president of the bank.

She'd been coming to this fair since she was a kid. Not much had changed. Some things, of course, had. There were more dinner options, you could now get a

Philly cheesesteak hoagie *and* a hot dog. You could still do the ring toss, and there was some sort of virtual reality game the kids were all lined up for. But the essence of the fair—the small town, neighborly feel of the event was the same as it was when she was the age Carson and Cash are now. Liv found a certain measure of comfort in that, but also a strange discontent.

She was ready for things to be different. Selling her house would fulfill that need, but somehow Liv knew that wouldn't be enough. Josh had opened her eyes—and her heart—to a bigger life. One not ruled by grief and guilt and secrets. If there was anything Liv learned this summer, it was this: while it may feel safer in the moment to keep her hard truths to herself, in the end, none of it was worth it. Her head turned from side to side again, searching. She wondered if it was obvious that she was looking for *someone,* not just looking around, but she guessed it didn't really matter. Seeing Josh would hurt, but not seeing him would hurt more. So she kept looking.

The line for the elephant ears was fairly long. She looked at her watch and guessed she'd be a little late for their meet up at the popcorn stand. She quickly texted Bella and told her where she was and that she would be along when she was done. When she reached over her shoulder to put her phone back into her purse, she missed and accidentally dropped it on the ground. The line moved up a notch as Liv leaned over to retrieve her phone. Inspecting her phone in her hand, she stood up and took a step forward without looking.

"Oh, excuse me," she said as she stepped into the chest of a man. And there he was, elephant ear in hand.

Josh.

"Josh …" Liv's voice was quiet.

"Hey, Liv. I'm sorry. I was just trying to get out of the way."

The two stared at each other for a moment. The noise of the games and the lights of the elephant ear cart were glaring and garish. But neither one noticed. Liv stepped forward as the line moved, and Josh followed. Liv looked up into his eyes. Her heart had gone from beating to pounding, and she felt her body flush and her cheeks turn pink. She'd been looking for him since she got to the festival, but now that he was here, she had no idea what to say. She couldn't tell him how she really felt; she'd made a promise to herself that she would put Bella first until her daughter was ready for her to move on, and she meant that promise. It wouldn't be fair to Josh—the push and pull. Still, the flush of her cheeks grew deeper as her eyes fell over his features. His long lashes, his coy smile, the length of his legs and the strength of his arms. The heat in her chest sunk deep in her body.

"No, it was my fault. I'm sorry. I ... I ah ... dropped my phone." Liv looked down at the phone in her hand, not sure what to say next. "How's your mom?" Liv asked, defaulting to the obvious.

"She's fine. She's here, actually." Josh tipped his head over toward the tent with tables lined for eating. He lifted the elephant ear in his hand and continued, "I'm taking this back to her. She loves them."

Liv smiled and said, "You're a good son."

"Is Bella okay?"

His concern for her daughter, even after the way she'd treated him, only served to make Liv feel even worse about letting him go. She took a deep breath. "She is. We are getting through. It's been a lot of work getting the house ready to sell and it's been good for us to do that together. This is ..." She motioned her hand between the two of them. "This is the right thing for me to do."

"If I have to give you up, then at least it's to your daughter."

Liv smiled, because even though her heart was breaking, looking at him made her happy. There was so much she wanted to ask him. A lot she wanted to say. But her voice betrayed her nervousness and her conscience—the one that reminded her that she needed to stick by her promise—and nothing she said would make this any easier. She had to let Josh go.

"Josh, I'm sorry."

Josh's lips tipped upward on the ends. He was smiling, but it didn't reach his eyes. Instead, he nodded his head in agreement. "I am, too."

"I wish I could …"

"The stars just don't seem to want to align for us no matter how much I want them to."

"I wanted them to," Liv whispered.

"I guess that will have to be enough. I'll always wonder what happens to you, Liv Harrison Pennington." Josh leaned down and brushed his lips gently across Liv's mouth. The sensation was so light, Liv feared she'd imagined it. She longed to reach up and kiss him again, to rest her head against his chest. She wanted to feel the beat of his heart, and soak in the warmth of his skin. Could the storm really have been only a few weeks ago? It felt like an eternity.

Josh ran his hand up and down Liv's arm and ended the touch with a gentle squeeze as he turned and walked away. Liv reached up and touched her fingers to her lips, feeling the moisture he'd left there. She took a deep breath and gathered herself, turning to watch him disappear into the crowd as if he was never even standing here in front of her at all.

Summer Love

The line for elephant ears was even longer now, and it had gone on without her. An elephant ear was the last thing she wanted, but she also didn't want to return to the group empty-handed. So she shuffled her way back to the end, stifling the smallest hiccup of a sob, and got in line.

Chapter 40

"She looks so … sad," Bella said, her voice lilting down just a touch at the end of her sentence.

"She is …" Lucy paused. "Sad."

"She really likes him, doesn't she?"

"She does."

Bella watched as her mom and Josh spoke. A sea of people slipped past them on each side. The line for elephant ears moved along without Liv. But neither her mom nor Josh seemed to notice—or care.

"She told me she wasn't seeing him anymore." Bella attempted to infuse her words with more contempt than she actually felt. Lucy turned and looked at Bella, tipping her chin down as her eyes cut straight to Bella's gaze. "What?" Bella asked.

"She isn't seeing him anymore. You know she's not. Your mom wouldn't lie to you about that."

"Except she lied to me about selling my house."

Lucy took an impatient gulp of air. "She didn't lie to you, Bella. She just didn't tell you the truth right away. That's different. And if memory serves, you gave her some pretty good reasons to believe you couldn't handle the truth."

Bella tried to respond, but there really wasn't an answer. Lucy was right. She wouldn't have been ready to hear about the house, and she'd acted like a brat most of the summer. It was no wonder her mom was leery of telling her about the house—or Josh.

Bella looked around to see if Maggie or Frannie were close by to overhear. She'd finished up riding the fair rides with Cash and Carson and met the ladies at the popcorn stand. Deciding she wanted an elephant ear too, Lucy offered to walk over to the stand with her.

Her dad had always been her go-to. He'd been the one to comfort Bella. He'd kissed her scraped knees and scared away the boogie men when she was too frightened to go to sleep. Losing him had felt like she no longer had a net. But that wasn't true. Her mom *was* her net. And while her mom chose a different way to show up for Bella, it still mattered. It mattered a lot. Her mom was the one to be sure her uniform was clean and to schedule doctor's appointments and to be sure that Bella had her homework done. It occurred to Bella suddenly that although her dad had been her go-to, her mom had been her anchor. She had created a foundation that Bella and Michael could safely live on without worry.

"I didn't ask her to stop seeing him, Lucy," Bella said.

"You didn't have to," Lucy answered.

Bella didn't know what to say. What could she say? Lucy was right. She hadn't asked her mom to stop seeing Josh. Her mom had done it because she knew Bella wanted her to.

"You're right. I didn't have to." Bella's voice was barely a whisper.

Bella took a step back out of the way of a passing group of middle-school-aged boys, but her eyes never left her mom. She watched as Josh gently bent and kissed Liv, a small chaste kiss, nothing sexy or embarrassing. A small, simple kiss that left Liv holding her fingers to her lips. And then, Josh was gone.

"He's a good guy, you know," Lucy said.

"How do you know?" Bella's words were said without a hint of sarcasm or judgment.

Lucy smiled at Bella and wrapped her arm around her shoulders, squeezing her into a hug. "I just do. You can trust me on this one."

Bella nodded in understanding as she watched Josh slip into the crowd of townspeople. His tall stature couldn't keep him from disappearing into the masses right away and Bella's eyes followed him until she couldn't see him any longer.

Bella had screwed up a lot this summer. And her mom—her mom had been there. Every step. *She* was the anchor. Watching her mom now, Bella saw a different side to her mother. The woman. The woman who'd been alone since her husband died. The woman who put her daughter first no matter what she needed for herself.

Shame crept up Bella's belly, and her cheeks flushed red. She'd spent the whole summer fighting her mother, and it was time for a white flag.

Chapter 41

"I thought you were heading to hang out with Hannah?" Liv asked as she poured the first glass of wine out of her favorite bottle of red.

"I was going to. But, I decided I'd rather come home. We don't have a lot of nights left to sleep in this house. I want to take full advantage of them." Bella smiled at her mom. A caramel apple scented candle burned on the kitchen counter, making the house smell like September.

"Are you hungry at all, sweet pea?" Liv asked.

Bella shook her head as she rubbed her belly. "I'm still full from all the junk I ate downtown."

"Me too." Liv laughed.

"Was your elephant ear good?"

"It was." Liv paused. Bella sensed her mom was thinking about Josh. "I have always loved them—Grandma used to get them for me." Liv shook her head from side-to-side. "I can't believe a) that festival has been going on so long, and b) that I'm still living in the same town I was when I was a kid. Crazy."

Bella laughed. "It is kind of crazy to live in the same town for so long. But I love it here in Blue Water Bay. I don't think it would be so bad to be here … forever."

Liv took her glass of wine and walked into the living room next to the kitchen, and Bella followed. Liv took a long sip of wine and stretched out on the chair in front of the fireplace, closing her eyes. Her hands wrapped around the stem of her favorite glass. "I would love nothing more than to be here forever. But I'm not sure that's in the cards. I am going to look at a condo in Franklin this week."

"You are? I didn't know you were going to buy something outside of Blue Water Bay …" Bella held her tone even, not wanting her mom to think she was angry. She was just … curious.

"Well, I didn't intend to. But Lucy thinks we can get a lot more bang for our buck up there. It's not too far of a drive, and you won't be living with me for too much longer—not that I mind. At all! I love having you here."

"Even when I'm a big brat?" Bella asked. She'd plopped down on the floor on her back near her mom's feet. She stretched her arms and legs as hard as she could before wrapping herself up in a small ball.

"Especially when you are a big brat." Liv laughed.

"Have you given any thought to what you want to do instead of school this fall?"

"I am going to keep working at Beyond Blooms. I love it there. I know it's not a career for me—I have a few ideas of some things I want to look into. I just really think I need some time to figure it out, and it's good experience."

"It is good experience. And Maggie loves having you there. You have time. Nothing has to be decided right away. When you're ready to talk about your options, I'd love to hear them."

"I promise I won't keep anything like that from you again, Mom. I'm really sorry I lied about school. And Hannah. And I'm sorry about Tequila Night, too."

"I know you are, sweet pea. And I'm sorry, too. I'm sorry I didn't listen. I will make you a deal. You tell me the truth, and I will promise to listen."

"Deal."

"To be clear, I'm not promising to agree with all your choices. Just listen to them." Liv's lips turned up in a smirk.

Bella laughed.

"Whenever I had big decisions to make, your dad used to say to me, 'Make the best decision you can with what you know today. That's it. And tomorrow if you know more, change course if you need to.'"

"He used to tell me that, too. I guess I forgot," Bella closed her eyes and took a deep breath. She'd been so worried about her mom forgetting her dad that she'd let pieces of him slip away. But remembering his advice now felt like a relief. There would be things she let slip and they would return when she needed them. It didn't matter if she remembered everything. What mattered is that she honored him. Bella knew exactly how to do that.

"I did, too." Liv took a sip of her wine.

Bella watched her mom as she looked out the window. Following her gaze, Bella was surprised to see she could see through the trees and up to the stars laced against the inky black sky from her angle. For the first time, Bella felt her dad's loss through the eyes of her mom. Yes, Bella had lost her dad. Her favorite person in the world. But her mom had lost her *person*. Bella had been so busy believing that losing her dad was harder for her than it was for her mom to lose her husband she hadn't stopped to realize it wasn't a competition. They both lost Michael. And they both had to find a way to keep living.

"Mom?"

"Yes, sweet pea?"

"I think you should call Josh."

Liv's eyes flashed toward Bella's. "What? What do

you mean?"

"I saw you. Talking to him in the elephant ear line. I saw him kiss you."

"Bella, it wasn't a real kiss. It was a ... goodbye kiss. Honest, sweet pea, I'm not seeing him anymore—"

"Mom? Didn't you hear me? I said I think you *should* call Josh."

Liv's breath quickened as her heart began to beat even faster. "But you aren't ready for me to ... you aren't ready for that yet. And you've had so many changes, I don't want to stack any more on you."

"But you like him. Like, really like him. And ... Lucy says he's a good guy."

Liv laughed out loud. "Well, if Lucy said it, it must be true. Right?"

"In this case, I will take her word for it. Well, that and the man did carry me inside after I drank too much tequila when he didn't even know me." Liv and Bella laughed, their voices dancing in and out together nearly as one.

"Are you sure?" Liv's voice was tenuous.

"I'm sure," Bella answered, nodding her head.

"What made you change your mind?" Liv took another sip of wine. Bella smiled as she noticed the slightest tremor in her mom's grasp. This was the right thing to do.

"To be fair, you never actually asked me if I was uncomfortable with you dating. I know I acted that way, and I'm sorry for that. I don't blame you for assuming I wouldn't like it. But tonight, when I saw you with Josh, I saw you smile. And I saw how sad you were when he walked away. And ... Lucy had a talk with me. You know how she tells it like it is. Well, she told it like it is." Bella took a deep breath and stretched again. "I don't want you to be sad, Mom. And I'm not worried about you forgetting Dad anymore, either. I know that will never happen. I should have never, ever been afraid of that to begin with."

"Never," Liv whispered.

"You're right. I'm not going to live here forever, and you shouldn't have to live your life alone—or miss out on a great guy because I miss my dad. The fact is I'm always going to miss Dad. In the beginning, I thought that was supposed to go away. Like, I was supposed to *get over it* or something, that there was a timeline to how long I could be sad. But now I know that it will always be a part of me. Not the biggest part or the only part, but a part of me. And I can't let that interfere with living my life or letting you live yours."

Liv interrupted her daughter. "I will always miss your father. He was my best friend and the love of my life and *your* father. In fact, I think that's where Josh made it easy for me to begin to … care about him. He has always asked about your dad and then really listened. He respects my love for your dad, he does. No man will ever take your dad's place. Ever. You have my solemn promise."

"I believe you, Mom. I should have never doubted that."

"It's okay, sweet pea. Grief twists us up and turns us around. It's all-encompassing and there is no manual they give you when someone you love dies. We just do the best we can. That's all we can do."

"I should have never doubted *you*. You have always been there for me. I should have remembered you always will, no matter what."

Liv set down her glass of wine and stretched out on the floor next to her daughter. She rocked her head up close to Bella's shoulder and rubbed her daughter's back in answer.

"Call Josh, Mom."

Liv nodded her head in agreement. Her eyes filled with tears as she lay on the floor next to her daughter. Bella took a deep breath and squeezed her eyes shut, saying a small prayer, *Please don't let it be too late.*

Chapter 42

Isla,

Good morning! Well, technically it may still be nighttime where you are. But for me, it's the early hours of a new day. The sun has yet to rise. In fact, it won't spread its light for several hours.

I wanted to tell you I'm sorry. I'm sorry for not being more responsive since Michael died. While I realize that may be not enough and a little too late, I need to offer it anyway. You have always given me your very best and I am a shade embarrassed and also very sorry that I have not given you that in return. I hold no animosity toward you; losing my contract was my own doing. You did everything you could to stop it, and I am grateful for that.

What I should have told you was that I was struggling. When Michael died, it was like my creativity, my ability to write, slipped from my fingers just as he did. I kept putting one foot in front of the other, trying everything I could to make it right. Honestly? I thought if

I just waited it out, it would come back. But it didn't.

Well, that's not entirely true. My words did come back to me, but not in the way I expected. I am sending you a copy of my newest manuscript, *The Last Sunrise*. It is the story of Michael and me. *Our* love story. I know it's not what I was contracted to write, nor is it what we have been successful in producing. But, I am hoping you will read it anyway.

Again, thank you for our business partnership, but even more so for the years of friendship we have had. I'd love to hear what you think once you've had a chance to read it, if you choose to.

All my Best,
Liv

Chapter 43

Liv had carefully packed her picnic basket with a small container of strawberries and two cinnamon rolls from The Local Cup. She'd also packed a bottle of Prosecco and two champagne flutes. She was hoping they would have something to celebrate.

The wind off the water and rising over the bluff had a distinct autumn chill. The day promised to be full sun and warm, but the early morning hours were definitely ushering in the next of seasons. Liv had been surprised at Bella's request that she call Josh. She had been so certain Bella was not ready for Liv to be involved with Josh—and frankly she still thinks she was right. She'd have to ask Lucy what she had said to her daughter to change her mind. While she was at it, she would thank her, too.

After Bella and Liv had talked, Bella headed to bed and Liv stayed up finishing her wine. She'd contemplated texting Josh, but decided she wanted to see him face-to-face. He deserved that much. He'd been a patient and understanding man for the past months, and she wanted to do more than tell him she was ready. She wanted to *show* him.

Plus, there were a few things left for her to do before she went to Josh.

It felt good to send her manuscript off to Isla. For some reason, her worry that Isla wouldn't like it didn't seem to matter anymore. Her fear that it wouldn't be good enough was gone. Something had changed. She changed, she supposed. She valued Isla's blessing, of course, but she was indifferent to Isla's feedback. The story, the story of Liv and Michael, deserved to see the light of day, and if Isla passed, Liv would find some other way. Lucy was right—she could help other women, and that mattered.

As good as it felt to send the manuscript off to Isla, it felt even better to give it to Bella. She'd left a copy on Bella's bedside table early this morning while her daughter slept. She'd left a note that simply said, *So we can always remember.* Liv tucked a lock of her daughter's hair away from her face and kissed her forehead. She had been afraid for months that she would lose Bella, but here in the dark, watching her sleep, she realized that no matter what, no matter how hard life got, they would have each other.

Now, Liv's tummy bounced with butterflies, and her hands were damp with perspiration. Starting over wasn't easy. Even thinking about all she and Josh had to navigate made Liv feel momentarily overwhelmed. Still, her excitement won out. Her manuscript had been sent, and she had Bella's blessing. She was hopeful. It was time to step back into the world full force. It was time for her and Josh.

She pulled through town, driving past The Local Cup and Beyond Blooms. The bike shop across the street was closed for the holiday, but she could see down the road at the main intersection that the marina was busy. People were scurrying around, cleaning their boats, packing cars, and getting ready to head home—some for the summer. Others for the workweek.

They would still have a few good weather weekends left. In fact, in some ways September was the best month to be in Blue Water Bay. The lake wasn't as full of boaters, and the colors on the trees made for a majestic view. Liv felt giddy at the prospect of a boat ride with Josh. They could go down to the Detroit River again, or maybe just anchor out in a bay like they had the first time. Either would be fine with Liv.

Liv pulled into the driveway and slowly rolled to a stop. She took a deep breath, attempting to tame the excited nervousness that settled in her belly in a way it hadn't for years, frightening but also sweet. She put the car in park and gathered up the picnic basket, taking both hands to lift it up and out of the seat.

The last time she was here, the air had smelled of freshly cut grass and the house looked a touch under the weather. But today, the grand house stood tall on top of its hill. The siding had been painted, and the emerald-green trim spruced up. The yard was immaculate, and the gardens had been weeded and cut back. Josh had been busy.

Taking a deep pull of the morning air, Liv closed her eyes and walked toward the front door. The steps were wide and welcoming. The boards looked new, as if they had been replaced also. The front porch itself looked different, although Liv couldn't put her finger on what had changed.

She looked down at her outfit—she'd tried on three before settling on a long, fitted maxi dress with a slit up the right leg with her short-cut jean jacket. It was a bright coral color, and the high neckline highlighted her thin neck. She'd dusted her cheeks with color and put on mascara. Her lips were plumped with lip gloss, and she felt beautiful. Strong. She rang the doorbell and waited.

A few minutes later, when Josh still hadn't answered, Liv's excitement began to turn to worry. She set her picnic basket down and rang the doorbell again. This time she clasped her hands together, her thumbs spinning in anticipation. Just because he didn't answer right this minute didn't mean he wasn't home, she reasoned. But that wasn't what she worried about. It wasn't that she was worried he wasn't *home*. It was that she was worried he'd gone *home.*

Looking around the porch, she realized what was different. Furniture. There was none. The last time she had visited there had been a love seat on the right side with cute cherry patterned cushions she'd noticed. And on the left had been two black rocking chairs that she and Josh had sat in. Fear shot through her like a dart. *She was too late.*

"Don't panic, Liv. Summer is over, and lots of people put their furniture up once the season is over," she scolded herself.

Walking slowly toward the floor-to-ceiling windows that lined the porch, she cupped her hands over her eyes and peered in. The windows were covered with sheer white curtain panels that gave her a hazy view. Everything looked to be in order. There wasn't a chair turned out of place, not a coat hanging on the rack or a pair of shoes by the door. The house looked lonely. Back at the door, she tried to twist the knob. Locked. No one locks their doors in Blue Water Bay. Not unless they were gone. Really gone.

Could it be that after all this time, their stars *still* wouldn't align? Were they destined to only have summer love?

The night they'd spent on Harmony Beach together came back in technicolor clarity. She could feel his arms wrapped around her and the warmth of his moist breath landing on her cheek. The fire crackled, and the air was infused with the sweet, smoky scent of burning wood. She had tried to memorize the sky, the pattern of the stars. She'd kept that memory tight in her chest all these years and now she supposed she'd tuck it next to a summer full of new memories and hold it longer.

Sitting down on the top step of the porch, she rested her elbows on her knees, tucking a rogue lock of hair behind her ear. Sure, she'd worried she was too late, but she had such high hopes it was a dim worry, one in the back of her mind that she didn't shed much light on. But now, it was clear. Josh was gone. She could call him, but should she? If he'd walked away from Blue Water Bay, maybe it was time they stopped trying to make "them" happen.

Liv's cell phone buzzed in the pocket of her jacket. Her hands shook as she pulled it out.

Lucy.

Liv took a deep breath before answering. "Hi, Luce.

What's up?"

"Good morning, Olivia!" she sang. "I have some really great news! We have a full-price offer! Cash!"

"We do? You haven't even shown the house yet … How did that happen?"

"I'm just that good, Olivia Pennington. Don't you forget it." Lucy's voice was full of laughter.

"Kind of hard to do when you won't *let* me forget it," Liv answered as a tear rolled down her cheek.

"I'm just leaving the office and can be at your house in fifteen."

"I'm … I'm not—"

"Where are you?" Lucy's voice dropped in enthusiasm. "Are you okay, Liv?"

"I'm fine." Liv stood up and looked around. The stars may not have aligned for Josh and Liv, but Liv would find a way for them to align for herself. Taking a deep breath, she answered, "I'll see you in fifteen."

Chapter 44

Liv ran her hand on the steel pipe railing as she walked down the steps of the bluff toward her beach. She held her long dress up with one hand, keeping it from dragging on the concrete steps. The trees had already taken on a dusting of faded green. They weren't quite changing color, but they weren't July-green anymore, either. Not quite summer, but not quite fall. Just like Liv felt. Somewhere in between here and there.

When she reached the beach, she pulled out one of the Adirondack chairs and dusted it off and sat down. The water was smooth as glass this morning, with only a ripple of waves to keep her company. Deep in the horizon she could see four freighters, two in the foreground and two so far out she would have missed them if she hadn't been looking. She hoped wherever she landed, she would have a view of the water, although she wasn't sure that would be possible money-wise. The view of the lake was nice, but it was the freighters she wanted to see. She took a deep breath and realized it really didn't matter if she could see them or not. She would know they were there either way.

She'd called Bella on the short drive from Josh's parents' house. When she'd told her about the full-price offer, her daughter cried. They'd both cried. It was what they needed, but not what they wanted. Wasn't life like that sometimes? Liv knew in the end, all that mattered was that Bella and Liv had found each other again and they were healing from the wound that losing Michael had left. Knowing the tender bruise of his loss would always be there comforted Liv, and also gave her the strength to move on.

She looked at her watch. Lucy should be here by now. It'd been nearly half an hour. Knowing Lucy, she was still sitting in her car in Liv's driveway, talking to a client on the phone. She quickly texted Lucy to tell her she was down on the beach, and before she could put the phone back down, it buzzed again, making her heart jump.

Expecting to see Lucy's name, she was surprised to see the screen say: Isla.

Isla: Liv! I happened to be up working when your email came in. I've read nearly all of TLS. It's your best work yet. Amazing. I just couldn't wait until I was done to let you know. I. Love. It. And I love you. Be in touch soon. But rest assured, I can sell this.

Liv wiped the tear from her eyes as it slipped down her cheek. Life was so funny sometimes. She was finally ready to have Josh in her life, and he had left Blue Water Bay. She'd finally broken through her writer's block, but too late to save her contract or her house. She supposed she could focus on what she'd lost, but instead, she looked out at the horizon and chose to focus on what she'd found.

The waves from the water rolled in, gently licking the sand. The sun had risen up over the waterline and was on a path straight into the sky. She'd missed sunrise this morning, but it had still happened. She had been devastated when Michael died, and even though she couldn't see her healing happening—it had. Liv had made it through a lot of hard times in the past two years. She would make it through more.

Lost in her thoughts, Liv closed her eyes and took in deep breaths of the fall air. Fall was a time for change. She had hoped she and Josh would make it to September, and beyond. They hadn't. But she had. She had so much to be grateful for.

"Liv?"

Afraid to turn around, Liv squeezed her eyes closed. "Josh?" she asked.

"I thought maybe you'd want your picnic basket back," he smiled, holding out the basket in offering.

Liv put her head in her hand. She must have set it down on his porch and forgotten it when Lucy called. "I just can't keep track of that thing, can I?" She laughed.

Josh put the basket on the sand next to Liv's chair as he pulled the second Adirondack chair over to join her. Dusting off the droplets of dew and a few stray leaves, Josh sat. Crossing his legs he leaned back, resting his head. He closed his eyes and took a deep breath.

So Liv did too. Liv expected silence. Instead she was awash with the sound of birds, lapping water, and the gentle breeze. The leaves from the trees, just starting to dry for their coming fall, were a shade louder than the height of summer.

Finally he spoke. "Since you took the time to pack a picnic, do you think we ought to eat it?"

Liv lifted her head and smiled. "Lucy will be here any minute." Liv looked at her watch. "In fact, I'm surprised she's not here yet."

"We have time," Josh answered. He opened the basket and pulled out the chilled bottle of Prosecco, then began the task of twisting off the muselet. "Why don't you get the glasses out while I open this?"

Liv reached into the basket and pulled out the champagne flutes. Her head tipped in question as she saw a key at the bottom of one of the glasses. Heat crept up Liv's chest and into her cheeks, burning her ears. She felt as if she should understand, but she couldn't piece together fast enough what was happening. She looked at Josh, her eyes asking him what was going on.

"Welcome home, Liv," Josh said as the cork shot into the air, landing on the sand just a few feet from them.

"What do you mean?" Liv's voice was barely a whisper.

"Just what I said. Welcome home." Josh poured one glass of Prosecco and then gently tipped the key out of the second glass and into Liv's hand.

Recognition hit Liv hard as she held the key. It was the key she'd given to Lucy to use to show the house. The spare key Michael always had hidden out in the garden behind the bird feeder. His initials, MP, were written on the front side. She shook her head again, turning the key over in the palm of her hand.

"I'm the full-price offer, Liv."

"Wait … what? You mean you bought my house?" Liv's voice went from a whisper to a roar. "You? You're going to live in my house?" Her brow pulled together in a fierce question, too much information was coming too fast.

"No." Josh laughed out loud and poured the second glass, then handed it to Liv. "You are. Well, you and

Bella."

"What are you talking about?" Liv pulled her glass close to take a sip, letting the sparkling bubbles tickle her face.

"I went to see Lucy last week about listing my parents' house. We got to talking and the idea came to me. I bought your house, but you can stay and live in it until the advance from your next book—or books—comes and you get back on your feet. When you're ready, I will sell it back to you for what I bought it for. It's an investment for me."

"It's not much of an investment if you only are getting back what you're putting in. I mean, I'm not an accountant and I'm not even very good at math, but that doesn't sound like a good deal for you."

"Money-wise, probably not. But it's an investment. In you."

"Josh, I can't let you do this. I can't. It's too much."

"I thought you might say that. Lucy did, too." Josh leaned back and took a sip of his bubbly. "So, let me ask you this. Why was your picnic basket on my porch this morning?"

Liv smiled and nodded. "Because I was on your front porch this morning." Liv watched as his long lashes fluttered, adjusting to the rising sun. His profile was strong, outlined against a clear blue sky. The longing deep in her body, the one that had begun to keep her awake each night, suddenly broke loose and washed over her like a sick-day fever.

"And you were there, why?" Josh's voice held a hint of laughter.

The heat inside Liv was making sentences hard to put together. Still, she looked at this man. The one who she had loved as a girl and was falling for as a woman. The one who had saved her house, even as he helped her save herself. "I was there because I'm ready, Josh. I'm ready to move on. I'm ready for … the stars to align." Her cheeks blushed with the thoughts of where this might go. She longed to kiss him again, to dive into the water and float cheek-to-cheek like they had after the storm. She wanted to wrap her legs around him and let the water hold them both afloat.

"Are you sure?" He set his glass down and leaned toward Liv, the searing look from his eyes burrowing into her heart.

"I am sure."

"What does Bella think?"

"Bella agrees."

"Then it's settled."

"But the house, Josh. It's too much." Liv felt her stomach lift in a flight of butterfly nerves.

"Listen, you're going to get on your feet. Your next book—it's going to sell. And when the time comes and you want to purchase it back ... it's yours. No strings attached. No matter what happens."

"Why are you doing this?" Liv's body quivered with desire and relief. Could she and Bella really stay here, in their home?

"I've been in love with you since I was nineteen years old. I wouldn't trade any of the detours we took to each other, otherwise we wouldn't have Bella, Lacy, or Zane. And you wouldn't have had almost thirty wonderful years with a great man. I have spent a lifetime waiting for the stars to align for us, Liv. I am a patient man." He laughed. "But enough is enough."

Liv let loose a small laugh that grew as the new reality swept over her. She could stay in her house. She had Bella back, and Josh, and she knew Josh was right, her new book would sell. Liv leaned forward, holding Josh's face with each hand, and kissed him.

"As much as I'd like to continue this, Lucy should be here any minute." Liv consulted her watch again.

Josh laughed, a hearty, bold belly laugh. "Lucy isn't coming."

Liv let out a smirk as she finally understood. "She isn't?"

"No, I was here earlier to deliver my news, but you

were gone already. I must have just missed you. I called Lucy to see if she knew where you were at. I didn't want to call you—I wanted to see your face when I told you. So, we decided Lucy would call and entice you home. When she called, she thought maybe you were at my house. I jumped in my car, headed home, and found … the picnic basket." Josh's lips turned up on both sides, lighting his eyes from the inside. "I owe a lot to this picnic basket. If you hadn't left it in my car that first night in the rainstorm, I wouldn't have had a reason to stop by."

"You would have found another reason," Liv teased.

"You think so?"

"I know so."

Liv shook her head at all that had transpired this morning. She would have to thank Lucy, although she was pretty sure Lucy was equally as happy that Josh and Liv were together *and* that Liv and Bella wouldn't be leaving town.

"I would stay here, on this beach forever if we could," Liv said. She took a sip of her Prosecco, wondering if he remembered saying the same words to her all those years ago on Harmony Beach.

"Let's see, we have Prosecco left, some strawberries, and cinnamon rolls. Is that enough to get you through … forever?" His eyes sparkled. *He remembered.*

Summer Love

"I think it's plenty to last until sunset," Liv said.

"Sunset? The water faces east. You can't see the sunset from here." Josh tipped his head in question.

"No, you can't actually see the sun going down. But you know it's happening. The sky turns violet, like someone is dimming the lights. Then it all turns a black, India ink color. You can't see the difference between the sky and the water; you just know they are both there. I actually like the sunset better in this direction. I can feel the Earth putting the day to rest. You have to trust its happening, and then wait for it to rise again tomorrow. You should see it sometime."

"The sunset? Or the sunrise?" he asked, his voice painted with anticipation.

"Both," she said without hesitation. "You should be here for both."

And with that Josh leaned forward and kissed his summer love under a September sun.

Acknowledgements

It shouldn't surprise you that I am a voracious reader. But what may surprise you is the fact that I *love* to read the acknowledgments at the end of a book. Before I published *Last Turn Home* in 2018, I would read the thank you and heartfelt words of authors at the end of their books and wonder what it would be like to have done what I always wanted to do—write a book. Their words of thanks to their agents and editors and publishing companies and family and friends gave me an inside look into what it would really be like to live my dream, and in many ways inspired me to finally do so.

Including acknowledgements is not a custom adhered to by many indie authors, but my books will always end with my words of thanks if for no other reason than we do not take many everyday moments to celebrate what we mean to each other and finishing a book—well it's a big reason to celebrate.

So, with no further ado,

Thank you Mo, Courtney, Kira, Rusti, and Tamara for reading early versions of *Summer Love* and offering me actionable, honest, and excellent feedback to help me flush out the stuffy corners of my story. Your help is invaluable to me —and so is your friendship.

Susie Poole—Can you believe we are on book number

FIVE together? You have become so much more than an editor (book cover designer, logo creator, blurb fixer, wizard of all things I need) you have become a very dear friend. Thank you for all you do for me. Someday, in real life, we will have that wine ... or margarita ... or take your pick!

Cathy Busdicker, thank you so much for your generosity in sharing pictures, memories, and the history of the "Blue Water Bay" area. And more importantly, for allowing me to use your cottage—one of my favorites homes I've ever had the pleasure of touring—as the inspiration for Liv and Bella's home. I hope I did it justice.

My family. The one I was born into, the one I married into, and the family I choose for my heart. Nothing could be done without you.

Eric, Cooper, Jackson, and Aiden. You are my why for every single thing.

In creating the character of Liv, a widow trying to put her life back together, I had the inspiration of dear friends who have lost their husbands and while I won't name names – your strength, resilience and grit inspired me. Thank you for living life forward and being a shining example of doing hard things. You know who you are, and I love you.

With Love,
Lara xo

Lara writes women's fiction and clean, wholesome contemporary romance novels that are set along the fresh coast of Michigan. She looks to real life for common truths and inspiration to tell stories about ordinary women who use everyday courage to create extraordinary lives.

Lara is an "almost" empty-nester who enjoys spending time with her boys and family, travel, fitness, hiking and sunshine, her husband of over 25 years, and her Labrador, Lulu (and not necessarily in that order!). She can make the perfect lemon drop martini and loves a good glass of Michigan wine.

Want to keep up with the latest news of upcoming books? Follow Lara on Facebook, Instagram, and Goodreads, or sign up for her newsletter to get all the news of upcoming books (and the occasional give away!) first!

LaraAlspaugh.com

Made in the USA
Columbia, SC
03 June 2022